# THREE WOMEN

# IT WASN'T MURDER

"My glass froster. It's a new gadget. It hasn't even been marketed yet, but I have a friend who helped design it and he gave me one."

"What does it do?"

"It's a chemical spray that makes cocktail glasses frosty."

"And?"

"And it also gives you a high if you squirt it in your mouth."

"And?"

"And if you squirt too much of it in your mouth it freezes your lungs."

"So you squirted a big dose at Monroe's lungs?"

"**I didn't squirt it, I told** *him* **to squirt it.**"

"But how could he be so stupid?"

"He's not stupid. Really, Freddy. You can be too insulting for words. He was just a little drunk, and I told him a squirt of the stuff would give him this really great feeling. Like he was flying. So he squirted it in his mouth and then we started to eat and his lungs froze and he strangled."

"But you didn't mean to kill him?"

"I didn't mean to kill him. And I didn't kill him. He killed himself."

We will send you a free catalog on request. Any titles not in your local bookstore can be purchased by mail. Send the price of the book plus 50¢ shipping charge to Leisure Books, P.O. Box 511, Murray Hill Station, New York, N.Y. 10156-0511.

Titles currently in print are available for industrial and sales promotion at reduced rates. Address inquiries to Nordon Publications, Inc., Two Park Avenue, New York, N.Y. 10016, Attention: Premium Sales Department.

# THREE WOMEN

Firth Haring

LEISURE BOOKS ❧ NEW YORK CITY

A LEISURE BOOK

Published by

Nordon Publications, Inc.
Two Park Avenue
New York, N.Y. 10016

# THREE WOMEN

**1**

Bootsie was sad when Monroe died, and the fact that he had gone in such an undignified way made her even sadder. He had choked to death on a piece of lamb. It was a death she had never wished for him.

He had an immensely chic funeral. "He would have adored all this," Bootsie told their friends. "It's just the way he would have wanted it." Her voice trembled a little as she turned from the handsome teak casket to Max Fried, a lawyer, but not one that she had ever used, professionally. "Max, darling," she said, resting a gloved hand lightly on his arm. "Thanks so much for everything. You've been a peach."

And indeed, Monroe, tucked in under a vicuña rug, his superb head in final repose upon a blue satin pillow, would have agreed, although Max did not agree that Monroe would have wanted to go in such style. It was typical of Bootsie not to know what Monroe would have wanted, typical of her to think he would have liked all this. But, it no longer mattered what Monroe wanted, so Max had done his best to make the occasion a success. Dependable as always, he had helped Bootsie plan the three-day program, had made all the arrangements, remembered all the details. Though he was the least of all that gaudy group gathered there for the occasion, he had proved himself to be what, in fact, he had always been, a true friend—perhaps the only one Bootsie and Monroe had ever had.

As she thanked him, Bootsie realized once again that it was his very helpfulness, his service, his true blueness that set him apart from her other friends, and she knew that they were wondering who he was —the helpful middle-aged Jew in the baggy suit whom they could only vaguely remember having seen at her parties, although he had been at many of them.

She patted his arm and moved on through the room and out onto the back verandah of the funeral home. The September evening was fragrant with chrysanthemums and asters. She stood at the verandah railing and looked down the hill toward the river, then up at the sky, which showed its stars over the chestnut trees. It had been a perfect day, she thought. If only the weather holds.

"Bootsie, baby."

She turned. "Freddy. How sweet of you to come."

"Baby. How awful for you."

"Thank you darling. I'm so glad you could make it." She touched his cheek tenderly, but a little distractedly, so it seemed to him.

"Are you bearing up?"

"Oh yes. It's been an ordeal. Thank you for coming."

"I was coming up anyway." He hadn't meant to say that. Now it sounded as if he wouldn't have bothered otherwise. "But I'll drive up again tomorrow," he said hastily. "Tomorrow's the funeral, isn't it?"

"Yes," she said, wondering why he had driven the thirty miles from the city if not to see her. "Tomorrow. I hope the weather holds. It would be dreadful if he had to be buried in the rain. Everything else has been so perfect."

Monroe's last day on earth was a glorious one. The sun shone brightly—so brightly and warmly, in fact, that Bootsie wondered if the vicuña might not have been, after all, inappropriate for a late summer funeral. There had been a nip in the air the day she bought it. But the temperature would drop at night, she told herself, and he would be glad to have the extra warmth.

As the cortege wound through the village on its way up the hill to the cemetery, it was evident that Monroe's passing had not gone unnoticed. Shopkeepers stood solemnly in doorways and pedestrians stopped to watch the long process of the limousines up Main Street. Bootsie snuggled back into the soft grey plush of the lead car, and smiled down at her young son Rodney, pale and tense beside her.

"It'll be all over in a little while, Roddy," she said, "Don't be blue."

Roddy started to cry.

"Now, darling, don't cry again. Please don't, or you'll make me cry."

Roddy crumpled against her. "Why did my Daddy die?" he sobbed.

"Now, darling, *please* don't. It was an accident, and we can't do anything about it. Daddy wouldn't

13

have wanted you to cry." She stroked his head and dabbed at her eyes with a lacey handkerchief. "Look, see the ball field! See all the boys." She had a tendency with the child to lapse into the cadences of Dick and Jane at times, as if he had not outgrown them years before. "See. See." But he was unconsolable. When they arrived at the cemetery, she sent him home with a neighbor.

After the ceremony, there was a collation at the house and, it being a Saturday and almost the cocktail hour, cocktails were served.

Bootsie, thinking back on it, wished her friends hadn't gotten quite so informal. After all, it was still part of the funeral, even though it happened to be a Saturday. She was glad that neither Monroe nor she had any family left to witness the scene.

Max arrived at the house before most of the guests and was at the door when they turned up. It was Max and Mrs. Johnson, both grim-faced, sober, dressed in black that might have been bought for a funeral a decade or more before, and the two solemn waiters (hired for the occasion) who gave the party its only funereal note. Even the laurel wreath on the front door seemed more an unseasonal symbol of Christmas than a notification of death.

There was shrimp to start, and oysters, and clams, and mussels. "All the little fishies we haven't had since April," said Marylou Harris to Max.

"Why not?"

"Mustn't eat shellfish in months without r's."

"Oh. Yes. They give off a chemical."

"Naughty man," she said. "Have a little fishie. It's been so long."

"Thanks, I've had a few."

"You're Jewish, aren't you?"

"Yes."

"I asked because I adore Jewish men. They're so warm and emotional."

"Are they?"

"Yes. They are. They really are. They're marvellous. I almost married one once. The reason I didn't was, was . . . Oh, I don't know what it was. It was just foreign, *you* know."

"Yes. I suppose it was."

"Do have a little fishie."

"No. Thanks, really."

"You're no fun," she said, popping an oyster into her mouth. "Were you a friend of Monroe's or something?"

"Something like that."

"How come I never met you before?"

"Well, I'm not much of a one for parties."

She nodded sympathetically. "I can see that," she said. "You're an introvert, aren't you?" Before he had to answer they were joined by Marylou's former husband, who sometimes got to take her home from parties, and Max took the opportunity to wander off to another position in the living room from where he could see Bootsie directing the waiters to start carving the turkey, the ham, and the roast beef.

"What a blast," he heard Ed Robinson say.

"The Osbornes always do things up brown." Max did not recognize the second voice.

"Did, you mean."

"Well, confidentially, I don't think things will change much."

"No, I suppose not. What do they say, the more things change the more they stay the same.

"Bootsie'll bounce right back."

Max wandered off toward the buffet table and

fixed himself a plate.

"Great party," someone said to him, as if he were the host.

"Great party," someone else echoed.

"Well, it's his last one."

"Whose?"

"Monroe's."

"Oh. Yes, poor devil. What was it he choked on, ham?"

"Lamb."

"Lamb. What a way to go. And in the pink of health, too."

Max found himself in Monroe's study with Freddy Turner, who did not recognize him, even though they had met just a few weeks before. "Yes, of course," he said triumphantly, his memory jogged by Max. "You're Monroe's golf buddy. Or, rather, *were.*" He shoveled a load of roast beef and potato salad into his mouth before moving over on the window seat to make room for Max. "Live around here?"

Freddy talked with his mouth full, and there was a speck of mayonnaise on his cheek. Max chose to remain standing. "I've lived here for twenty years." He wished he had not come back to the house after the funeral. He wished he were with Louise now, kind tolerant Louise, who would listen to him speak of his dead friend and who would try to understand something of the strange bond that had existed between the two men: the small-town Jew and the cosmopolitan Gentile (a paradox in itself, since Max had grown up in the Bronx and Monroe in the little town where he had died). Though he was only a dozen years older, Max had felt like a father to the younger man. He had understood the nature of

Monroe's marriage better than Monroe himself had understood it, and at the same time he had had for Bootsie a compassion that Monroe was incapable of.

"It's not much of a town to spend twenty years in," Freddy was saying. "Although Bootsie seems to like it."

Max, who hardly ever disliked anybody, said stiffly, "Everybody who lives here likes it or they wouldn't live here."

"Monroe never liked it."

"Of course he did."

"No. He lived here for Bootsie."

"You've got it all wrong," Max said. "Bootsie and Monroe both grew up in this town and they both loved it. Bootsie grew up in that house right over there. You can just see it through those trees."

"Listen, friend," said Freddy, taking out his pipe. "Let me tell you a thing or two about Monroe. He got away with murder all these years. Whoring around the way he did."

"You don't know anything about it," Max said, suddenly hating Bootsie's smug, overfed defender.

Freddy set down his plate and stood. "I'm not one to speak ill of the dead," he said, strolling across the room, "but the guy didn't deserve a send-off like this." The door slammed behind him.

Oh, Louise, come to me, Max muttered.

He sank onto the window seat and sat in the dark staring out into the night, thinking of Bootsie and Monroe. They had married for the wrong reasons and they had stayed married for the wrong reasons. Bootsie, determined not to marry, as her friends had, comme il faut, had "discovered" him in her own world yet not in her world at all, had loved the unorthodox in him that she believed enhanced her

17

own uniqueness, and had fit him into her stars with no ado at all.

Freddy was right, of course. Monroe had never let her forget that she had deceived him, captured him. He had been so happy, wallowing contentedly in his uncomplicated bachelorhood. Like a gratified crocodile sunning itself on the banks of a warm river, he had sunned himself in a June of her smiles unconscious that by Independence Day the ropes of responsibility and duty would bind him. And then he understood: in return for her favors, he was to pledge a lifetime of love and service. The tears he had shed at that realization had not been crocodile tears, but real tears of regret for his lost freedom. However, when he had finished with them, he had submitted. And then, poor beast, he had discovered, only too late, that his tamer did not really "love" him—or in other words did not love him as he thought he deserved to be loved. She had only wanted to have him.

From beyond the dark, silent library came sounds of hilarity. The library door burst open, framing Bootsie's blond curls in the light for an instant. "Anybody here?" She slammed the door again before Max, still deep in his thoughts, could answer. He stood and smoothed out his clothes, then sadly left the room where he had sat so often with Monroe to see if there was anything he could do, now that Monroe was having a funeral.

The first thing he noticed when his eyes had adjusted to the light was that Bootsie was curled up in the soft goose-down couch with Freddy, and that Freddy was holding her hand. You lousy corpse hopper, Max thought.

"Hi, there," said Marylou Harris. "Where have

you been hibernating, you old bear you?"

(Marylou, you old bag you, don't set your cap for me. I am marrying Miss Louise Schade, and I would be very happy today if only my friend Monroe hadn't choked on a piece of lamb.)

"Well, hi," he said.

"I've been looking all over for you," she chirped. "Did you have enough to eat, honey?"

(Marylou, I am a Jew.

Marylou, don't be blue.

I am a Jew without a sou.

Don't be blue, you old bag you.)

"Yes, thanks. I've had plenty."

"I must say," she said coyly, "for a big man, you can certainly make yourself pretty hard to find."

"Well, I don't stand out in a crowd, I guess," he said.

"Now, *there* you go again. Being an old introvert. Why don't you try to build yourself up once in a while. Develop your ego. Stand up for your rights. I bet you come from a large family of brothers and sisters."

"Yes," he said, "I do, as a matter of fact."

"I knew it. I knew it the minute I met you. I was a sosh major in college and I wrote my senior thesis on kinship patterns. Now if there's one thing I learned it was that. . ."

"Marylou, darling, I know you're about to put your pitch over the plate, but do you mind if I take him away for a sec?" Bootsie appropriated Max's arm and led him off without waiting for Marylou's answer.

"Not if he promises to come right back," they heard her shout as they made their way through the din.

19

Back in Monroe's den, Bootsie said, "I didn't really want you. I just wanted to get you away from Marylou. You looked so uncomfy!"

"Thank you, Bootsie," he said sadly, "I was uncomfy." Why did he shift into her language when he was with her? "I can't stop thinking of Monroe."

"Oh, there now," she said, kicking an elephant's foot, her Christmas present to Monroe one year, bought at Brooks Brothers. "Don't be depressed. It's better this way." She smoothed the skirt of her black linen dress and sighed. She seemed anxious, and far away.

"What do you mean?" he asked.

"Hmmmm?"

"What did you mean it was better this way. Was he sick or something?"

"Oh, no. No, I didn't really mean anything. It's just the kind of thing you say when somebody dies, you know." She closed her eyes and leaned her head against the fieldstone fireplace. "Oh, Max," She said, "I can't believe it's all over, that I'll never see him again." A tear slipped down her cheek.

"Bootsie,"He dropped to her side. "You must rest. This has been too much for you."

Then, from somewhere in the house came the sound of an electric guitar.

"Who the hell turned that on?" He was furious. "I hate to say it, Bootsie, but your friends are a bunch of barbarians."

Before she could reply he had gone off in search of the offending machine. Bootsie rose and stretched. She couldn't really blame them. There was an honesty about her friends. They were honest toward life. They lived life the way they felt like living it. And now they were showing they could be honest toward death in accepting it for what it was: simply another fact of life. They had their own morality—a morality of license rather than one of discipline. It was her morality. Thou shalt not do anything you don't want to do. Thou shalt do anything you do want to do. Thou shalt put no other gods before thy ego. It was the new way, and when it came up against the old way—the way that said you couldn't always do what you wanted to do because there was something higher in the world than the ego that boomed No—a peculiar shudder was felt, the shudder of two planets bumping in the void, the shudder that produced "Barbarians!" at the sound of a frug at a funeral, the shudder that denied, at the same time as it recognized, a new spirit awaft in the universe. She relaxed out of her stretch into a languid shimmy or two—her partner her own reflection in the picture window—and then the music stopped.

Max was not the last guest to leave the house that night. The last guest stayed for breakfast, a fact Max discovered on Sunday morning when he drove past the Osbornes on his way to pick up the paper and saw Freddy's perky little Triumph parked next to the propane tanks, just where it had been the night before.

**2**

After Bootsie made it clear that she was not in the mood to go to bed with Freddy, he sat up and listened to her talk about herself all night.

She was virtue itself, she told him, if one judged her by her own standards. She lived as deeply a moral life as any nun, though her morality was of another hue. The path she trod was as straight as her sister Vivian's, a missionary to the Chinese in Hong Kong. Daughters of a military man, they had learned obedience early. They marched to his tune, whose lyrics had a hundred opening lines. Honesty is the best policy. To thine own self be true. Great oaks from little . . . . Actions speak louder . . . .

At a point in their lives, the girls veered away from each other, but not away from the philosophy of their father. They went in opposite directions, but both bowed as compulsively as a dowsing fork in the Jersey Pine Barrens to the source of that philosophy. In life, both found their energy at the same spring. That the energy took different forms was a matter of interpretation. For Vivian to be true to her own self she must serve others; for Bootsie she must serve herself.

The father had a blind spot. It is not clear whether the blind spot had caused him to go into the military, or whether the military had caused the blind spot. It was probably the former, however, since Bootsie had inherited it from him. Though in his own eyes and the eyes of his family and associates he was the epitome of moral rectitude, he had never been able to make sense of the golden rule. That was his blind spot, not that it was, in the least, a detriment to his career. If anything, it had hastened his ascent to Admiral. To do unto others as he would have them do unto him was sheer idiocy. Wars weren't won by sentimental crack-pots. In life, girls, God helps him who helps himself. Put your shoulder to the wheel.

His was a medieval world. A great chain of being passed from God in the firmament to the President in the White House to the Secretary of the Navy to the Admirals, to the Lieutenant Commanders to the ensigns, right on down to the Philippine mess boys in the galley. And as God was above the President and the President above (though in cahoots with) the defense establishment, so in ordinary (i.e., civilian) life was he, an Annapolis man and moreover a descendent of the valley's earliest settlers, above all those of lesser birth and achievement.

In Bootsie's own chain of being she was well near the top, but she had some of the starch taken out of her when she went away to college and tried to direct the girls she met there. In the twinkling of an eye she grasped the new fact. It could not be said that democracy came upon her. Rather oligarchy.

There were five of them, and united they stood. They sunned in the windows of their dorm, listened to Harry James. They polished their nails ruby red, played bridge, tried to sex up the male instructors, spent endless hours weaving fantasies about them. They were obsessed with marriage, talked about it all the time. But there was no one to marry. The college boys they dated they considered babies; the veterans one saw from a distance on neighboring campuses didn't date, and the five wouldn't have wanted to go out with them anyway. Senior by a few years and a war, they were as good as from another world, and funky with college girls. Besides, the G.I.'s thought engineering looked like a good field to get in to. If Elsbeth, Cissie, and Bootsie, all English majors, knew one thing it was that they had to marry English majors. They couldn't stand the thought of going through life with a husband who mightn't understand their literary allusions. Yet Monroe when she met him didn't even know what a literary allusion was. "Tell me about him," Freddy said. And she needed no urging. Monroe. When she married him he had just started his construction business. "My father wanted me to marry a military man. Monroe's two years in the Pacific didn't count, of course, even though he had a few scars scattered around his body to show for it."

"He wore blue pin-striped suits, double-breasted whether that style was in or out, and fedoras, and mahogany cordovans. He bought himself a camel's hair coat that first winter. A good one. It cost him two hundred and fifty dollars. It was down around his calves. The New Look." Bootsie made a drink for herself. She remembered how she had been taken by that coat, and by his black hair combed sleekly across his forehead. She was taken, too, by his dark glittering eyes telling her he did not go for her girlish chatter. No, he did not want to listen to her rave on about her precious intellectual college friends. There were only three years difference in their ages, but he seemed a generation older. "Does that mean you won't take me to Cissie's party?" "Does it really mean that much to you?" "No, I guess not." "We'll go, baby. We'll go." "But Monroe. You're rich, you're successful. Why should you care what they think of you?"

Freddy, stretched out on the couch, stirred. "Didn't they like him?" "They did. He had something their husbands didn't, and they knew it. He had an animal power, a finesse. People looked at him rather than at me when we went into a restaurant together or a night club."

She blew softly on the ice cubes in her glass, thinking of him. Monroe. He was a country man, though not a rustic. He was a burly man, though not very tall. He was a polished man, though not educated. He had chubby cheeks, a barrel chest, short thick legs, dimpled thighs, a pot belly. He was hairy, he shaved twice a day and he could drink a fifth of scotch and drive home. He could waltz, which none of her friends' husbands could do, and he had his own private squash court, built in a white rage when his application for membership in a club in New York was turned down. Whether waltzing, playing squash or making love, he perspired and gave off a rank, musky odor that she found both repellent and agreeable, like the perfume of a skunk.

Monroe. If a man can have a color, his was midnight blue, the color of the silk dressing gown he wrapped around himself the night he first made love to her. He was a man who could cherish, and that hot July night he had cherished her. He lived alone in a twelve-room house on sixty wooded acres, thirty years before a rich man's farm. In the morning she woke before him and rose on her elbow to observe him. It was already as hot as any August afternoon, and he lay naked sleeping on his back with the sheet across his thighs. His lips were parted, but he was not snoring. His short thick eyelashes quivered and sweat gathered on the bridge of his nose. She looked around the room. It was windowed floor to ceiling on south and east and a screened sleeping porch flanked the north. Cabbage roses trellised the walls. For Monroe it was bedroom, living room, work room, and kitchen. The kitchen was all neatly arranged on a card table in one corner. In another corner an oak roll-top desk and a steel filing cabinet contained the records of the Osborne Construction Corporation. Even though it was not yet eight o'clock, she could hear the bulldozer and chain saw far away through the woods clearing ground for Monroe's instant neighborhoods, a concept he was proud to have introduced to the rural county. The air that morning was full of the cries of the birds whose nests were being plundered by the machine.

He was the only man she had ever known well enough to kiss who had hair in his ears. She stealthily extended a forefinger and touched the tragus of his ear to feel these little hairs. He woke immediately. "What were you doing?" "Inspecting your ear." He opened his arms and she crept into them. Later, as they rode out in his jeep to see the construction, he sang "Stay as sweet as you are" at the top of his lungs.

It had been his experience that most women did

not stay as sweet as they had been.

Bootsie decided that day as she watched him striding over the denuded land, the sandy soil of the area already lightening and crumbling in the heat of the sun, the massive oaks and hickories felled to the right and to the left of her, granite boulders too large to be moved becoming the stations where the refuse of the operation was deposited, that he was a man who could make her happy. And he would have made her happy, too, if he had not turned against her in the early days of their marriage. He had never forgiven her for what was merely an honest answer to a not-so-simple question.

"What was the question?" Freddy. She had almost forgotten he was there.

"He asked me why I married him."

"And?"

"I told him a fortune teller had told me to because he was a perfect foil to my blonde beauty and impulsive temperament."

"And that bothered him?"

"He asked me if I hadn't married him because I loved him, and I said I did love him but I loved myself more, and he was good for my image. That's what bothered him. But I was just being honest."

"Don't you know honesty is the worst policy?"

"I always thought it was the best."

"Then be honest. Wouldn't you like to go to bed with me tonight?"

"No, I would not. I would like to go to bed alone tonight and weep for Monroe. You may sleep on the couch and cover yourself with my hand-made cashmere afghan and dream erotic dreams about me."

"Thanks, I'll do that," he said. "Good night, Bootsie."

**3**

When Max arrived at Louise's house the next morning, Helen was up on a stepladder, feather dusting the living room molding.

"Working so hard so early in the morning, and a Sunday at that, Helen?"

"What's Sunday got to do with it? I've already been to church." She climbed down off the ladder, dragged it a few feet and climbed up again to get at another section.

"I should think you'd sleep late on Sunday," he said. "It's your only day to."

"I never miss a Sunday at church," Helen said sternly, "which is more than can be said for some people." She swatted at the molding with her duster.

"I'm a hypocrite," said Louise. "I go only on Christmas and Easter."

"It's duly noted in the congregation," said Helen. "And elsewhere too," she added darkly.

When they had gone laughing off into the morning, Helen climbed down from the ladder. She hadn't meant to work today. She had only started to make Louise feel guilty for going out with Max again.

She could not get used to having him around, to having a man come into the house and take Louise away. It was something new, and disturbing. It had all started just a few months before, but it showed no sign of tapering off. How can it be, she asked herself, that he's been here in this town all these years and we never once laid eyes on him—only saw his name in a gilt arc on a second-story window above the jewelry store on Main Street? Max Fried. And underneath his name the six gilt letters spelling lawyer. It had meant nothing.

Max and Louise had asked each other the same question a dozen times. How is it we've both been here all these years and we never met till a few months ago? "And how is it that neither of us has ever married and yet now, now that we've met, marriage is all we think about?"

"And at our age, too."

"There's no fool like an old fool."

"Oh, we're not all that old."

She smiled at him. "*We* don't think so, but that's what people will say."

"Have you told Helen yet?"

"No. No, I haven't told her yet." How can I tell Helen, she wondered. The leaves of the maple trees bordering Broadway, the long residential street connecting her house to his apartment, already were turning yellow. She had put off telling her for a month. There was no point in telling her till she was sure that it was going to come off. She *would* feel an old fool if she told her and it didn't. But it could not be put off much longer. "I'll tell her this week," she said.

For twenty years, they had lived together in easy enmity at the foot of Prospect Street. In two decades of keeping house, they had never ceased to be surprised that they were still together. They had gone along, day by day at first, then month by month, then year by year, half expecting the whole arrangement to come to an end at any turn. In fact, the arrangement had come so close to ending so often—and the scene had been rehearsed in their respective imaginations so carefully—that Louise, for one, was perfectly confident that she could gather about her the accoutrements of all those years and clear out before sundown . . . leaving Helen to deal with the lawyers, the real-estate agents, the utilities companies, and the ear that Louise would blister before leaving. It was a scene that had fortified her for fully twenty years, compensating her for twenty years of her diminutive sister's bullying. She dwelt with sweet relish on the thought of that moment when she would clasp her brown felt on her grey bun, straighten her tweed lapels and stride off the porch in her polished oxfords to a waiting cab. She often recalled fondly the three sunny rooms on Lexington Avenue and Sixty-third Street that she had occupied for $34.50 a month for two years in the early forties and yearned defiantly, if vaguely, to be mistress of her own parlor once again.

She had enjoyed those years of bachelorhood on Lexington Avenue and had enjoyed during them a certain popularity with an earnest arty few culled from the acquaintances of her college years and her associates at the museum. She had entertained on occasion in paisley lounging pajamas and a green

35

turban and had smoked Danish wiffs and flicked her ashes into a blue china urn. She had taken a sociology course at the New School and had stuffed envelopes on Thursday evenings in the chilly quarters of the Socialists on Second Avenue. She had had a crossword puzzle published in the *Times* but had had less luck with a dozen sonnets in the style of Edna Millay. And for six months in 1941 she fed and sheltered a splendid actor fellow who wept nightly on her handsome breast and who departed one day in an autumn rain for Florida.

The following autumn, in her twenty-fifth year, she journeyed to the village that had nourished her to follow her father's coffin up the gravelled path to the Schade family plot, and had never returned to the city. There on the windy hill high above the river, the green and white courses of the cemetery, the nodding geraniums, the cry of the blackbirds, the trees swaying in the west wind, the bowed black shoulders of her father's friends bespoke a truth more urgent to her soul than the New York hash of art and parlor communism. She returned to the house on Prospect Street and hung up her hat. Helen, to whom the death had briefly represented the first chance she had had in twenty-seven years to get away from the house, was thus shamed into staying on.

At first, it was to be a temporary arrangement. After a decent interval they were to sell the house and take separate apartments, buy a car, and commute to interesting jobs in the city. They were to have the best of both worlds: city jobs and city friends, country air and a country perspective. But the dearth of buyers interested in a white elephant in need of a paint job and a new roof, the neat little income from their father's well-invested savings, and Louise's love of ease combined to thwart these plans. Helen found herself operating the switchboard at the local U.S.O. Club instead, and Louise, soft, plodding, vague Louise, took the position left vacant when the postmaster went off to the war.

Thus, for three years they did their patriotic duty and put off going their separate ways. "After the war" became a way of saying, "We'll sell the house and start living properly; we'll break up this queer marriage of ours and be rid of each other." That was what it had turned into—a queer marriage, which neither would be the first to dissolve, Louise out of sheer laziness—she had grown softer and more languorous on Helen's cooking—and Helen, poor Helen —who always misinterpreted Louise's motives— simply out of fear of being any less obedient than her sister to what she supposed were their dead father's wishes.

Driven by guilt, harassed by duty, Helen's blood ran cold to recall how ready she had been as his death seemed imminent to leave it all: to sell the house (even to strangers), to quit the village, to give up, in effect, her birthright. She paled now at the thought of how close she had come to leaving Louise, soft, pliable Louise, to her own resources, or worse, to the resources of the world. With the passing years, she had grown convinced of the rightness of doing things right—of doing them the way her father, and her mother, would have wanted them done—of, in other words, holding the family, such as it was, together. Her only regret was that it ironically had not been she who had instigated their ménage à deux. She ached to remember that it had been Louise, vague, intellectual Louise, who, unhampered all her life by "family feelings," had risen to the occasion with a noble show of daughterly devotion; Louise who had sacrificed her independence; Louise who had lighted the path of duty; Louise upon whom their father no doubt smiled from some heavenly abode. Poor Helen, her breast nearly burst to think back on her life's one moment of rebellion and to estimate what jewels in her heavenly crown she had forfeited by that brief infidelity. Even while she had raged at the promise she had given her father on his deathbed, the promise not to marry out of the church (that is to say, the Congregational Church), Louise had probably been forming, as if for spite, her felicitous decision. Helen did not for a moment imagine that this decision, which had caused her so much pain, had been conceived in Louise by a fleeting nostalgia, born of a temporary revulsion to the noxious city, the crowded buses, and the cockroaches and soot in her apartment, and nurtured by a habitual laziness. That her promise had nipped fairly in the bud the once welcome attentions of a certain Mr. Frank Petroiani, local attorney, seemed to Helen, in retrospect, ancillary to the loss of grace she believed she had suffered by her short-lived defection.

Portly but crumbling, the house that they had grown up in and had found so difficult to disencumber themselves of occupied an acre of weeds at the very end of Prospect Street—a street on which, as Louise once remarked, there were very few prospects. On one side of the house, the side going up the hill toward Broadway, there flourished Bender's Funeral Home, a buff and sepia establishment the very incarnation of decorum. On the other side, sliding off into the river, there existed nothing but a perishing sandstone seawall and, beyond that, three miles of rough grey water. A faded sign, erected by the town board at the height of a summer polio scare, read "Water Polluted: No Bathing" and staggered on the seawall within eye range of their dining room table. The bridge, the much-hated bridge that had leapt the grey water in 1955, was—its only saving grace—not visible from the house. A pier once useful had been nearly destroyed in a September hurricane. For years it had gathered seaweed and barnacles upon its rotting timbers.

A porch wavered unsteadily along the front and river sides of the house, and from it they had watched the seasons come and go, and rocked away the years. The river, at their juncture, bustled with small craft, which dipped and bobbled in and out of sight from a marina to the north and the cove of a boatyard slightly to the south, beyond the public park. The park itself swarmed with children at certain hours of the day and so, although their house was set somewhat apart from the town, they were by no means isolated from it. Indeed, the town nodded to them from the masts of tacking sailboats and occasionally waved to them, with an unidentifiable red or blue mitten, from the sliding board in the park.

Over the railings of the wicker and rattan-furnished porch with its faded chintz-covered glider and slatback rocker they had flicked, in and out of unison, the butts of thousands of cigarettes. When the dishes were done and the towels hung over the stove to dry, when the cruet and the saltcellar, the mustard pot and the cut-glass vase with its bouquet of frail silver spoons were replaced on the enamel tray where they had stood for fifty years, the sisters left the odors of the kitchen for the cool evening breezes on the porch and sat, usually in silence, until it was time to fold their newspapers and their sewing and climb to their rooms under the mansard roof. If they sometimes forgot to say good night, no matter. They would meet again in the morning in the uncarpeted upstairs hall on their way to the ill-heated bathroom with its leaded windows, linoleum floor, and claw-footed tub. The lugubrious flush of the chain-and-tank toilet and the whine of the faucets as they unwillingly gave up an inadequate trickle of rusty water could also be counted on, winter or summer.

There was little to distinguish the seasons from one another at 21 Prospect Street. In the spring, a chestnut tree bloomed outside of Louise's window and morning-glories climbed green cotton strings between the porch railing and the eaves of the porch roof to provide a screen for the two ladies as they rocked in the summer twilight. In summer, flyswatters, buckled and frayed, lay about the house, and balls of cotton, white as snow in May and begrimed and sodden in August, bobbed on the screen doors as a deterrent to flies—a household hint that Helen had learned from her mother and that was not taken by the flies. The screen doors, like the swatters, were warped and buckled.

In winter, snow lay on the roof outside their rooms and they could see from the upstairs windows the floes of ice whirling down the river. The windows rattled in their sashes and occasionally a shingle blew off the roof and spun across the backyard to land like some weird octagonal vegetable in the garden's crop of dirty snow. Aside from these minor events, aside from the occasional broken eggcup or the milkbottle found upset on the porch by a stray cat, the seasons had passed, not unnoticed, but rather, unheeded for twenty years.

The questions the girls sometimes asked themselves as they sat rocking on the porch, were not, Does anything lie in store for us? or, Is Life simply going to pass us by?, not these, because the answers to these were clear. Nothing *did* lie ahead; life *was* going to pass them by. The questions they asked were, Why does nothing lie ahead? Why have we let this happen to us? And they questioned neither emptily nor bitterly, but wonderingly, searching for the answers in their childhood, their dead parents.

The answer for Helen, although she could not articulate it, was fear. Neither could she articulate what it was that she feared. She knew only that a pervasive dread had dogged her all her life: a nameless dread of losing a nameless treasure; a wordless misgiving that fostered a silent doubt; a disquietude of the soul never pronounced; an ever-present apprehension, of what she knew not. She seldom attempted to identify it, to define it, to examine it. She simply accepted it, for the most part, as one accepts a birthmark, or a club foot; nevertheless, she had never learned to live on terms with it. It plagued her; it ruled her. It drove her to torment others as she herself was tormented. It goaded her on in her search for security. It tempted her to circumscribe the finite, to bind the already bound.

The years did not mellow Helen. As she grew older, she became more rigid, demanding of Louise the obeisance that her own fears demanded of her. And because Louise, to keep the peace, usually complied, it was not until Max Fried made his appearance in Helen's world that she found a suitable object for the anger she had stored up in herself for

41

forty-odd years.

Helen was not meant for men. She was not made for love. Louise, on the other hand, big, soft, languorous Louise with her jolly laugh and her bouncing bosom seemed just the type men liked. Yet, for Louise, as for her sister, the answer to why life had passed her by lay also in fear, a fear of the life that stirred so ominously within her and beckoned so invitingly from just beyond the garden gate.

She had been pretty in her bloom, though always on the large side. As a girl, it was her femininity, her softness, her jollity, her laughing face, her female docility, her young body bursting the seams of her serge school dresses, that had accounted for her surfeit of beaux and that had always seemed to irritate her mother, who distrusted femininity on principle.

Louise had in her soul a spark of adventure whose origin no one could account for. But the spark turned out to be only a spark after all. At seventeen, she overheard a conversation between her mother and an aunt from the Illinois Schades, who journeyed once a decade to visit her brother on the Hudson. "Louise is different from the other Schades, Martha." Was it a reproach, or was it a compliment? Louise, poised at the top of the stairs, feared it was the former.

"Yes, she's different." The clicking of her mother's knitting needles accelerated.

A silver spoon was set upon a china saucer. "Does she take after your side, Martha?"

"No one on my side."

"Well, I like her," said the aunt emphatically. "There's not a bit of Schade in her."

Her mother clicked on. "No, she's not a Schade."

"More power to her, I say," said the aunt, who,

though a Schade, had always counted it a bit of bad luck. "She's full of fun and she's got a mind of her own."

"Yes," said her mother, who disliked extravagance and sensed her sister-in-law waxing extravagant, "just the type who'll throw herself away some day."

In Louise was born that day a caution.

And thirty years later as she rocked alone on the porch she had the grace to wonder if it really would have been so bad after all—to have thrown herself away.

As they sped along the blacktop, the long lawns of the residential district rolled away from them bowl fashion on both sides of the road. The gables, cupolas, porches, towers, and gingerbread of the houses she knew so well flashed and fragmented in the sun. Fractured by the progress of the car, they danced in pretty profusion behind their screens of foliage. Yet, the stability and orderliness, the very tradition of conservatism they represented, denied, she knew, their fracturing by sun and by Max's quick "progress" up their way. It was not they that were fractured. They were there forever. Nothing could destroy them. Louise Schade's marrying a Jew would not affect them in the least. They would go on as before, simply forgetting about Louise Schade.

Max turned in at his driveway. The granite gate houses, sentinels themselves, needed no keeper to discourage the curious from approaching the great house. And the unkempt lawns, the unweeded beds needed no gardener to call attention to the fact that they had been planned and shaped by a staff of gardeners. The base was there: the form, the layout, the expensive perennials, the lily pond, the

43

fountains.

Max's apartment was on the second floor, in the rear, looking out over the river. Its French windows, all facing east, opened out onto a flagstone patio that ran along the width of the house in the back; beyond the patio was the meadowy lawn, the bank of yews and, beyond them, the river. The room was long and spacious, comfortably furnished and dim, in the afternoons, with an eastern light. There were a fireplace, couches situated around it, Oriental rugs, a grand piano, lamps, books, tables. At the other end of the room, behind a Japanese screen was the double bed to which Max and Louise now repaired.

They were not the lithe, athletic lovers of the cinema; rather, with their bulk and the slow, rolling motion of their copulation they resembled more a couple of bears grappling in some grim and important death hold. The very room shuddered with their agony. When it was over, they fell into the light, peaceful sleep of after love—their struggle mutually resolved. But they did not sleep for long. Max woke first and Louise soon after. She lay in his arms, considering herself fortunate. He was restless.

"You're upset about Monroe."

"Yes."

"How was the funeral?"

"It was big." He heaved his burly body up out of bed and padded across the room for his cigarettes. "It was big."

"How is Bootsie?"

"Bearing up." He thought of Freddy and wondered if Monroe had known.

"It was a terrible tragedy. Even though I hardly knew him, I felt awful. . . . Mostly because of you,

44

though." She stroked his hairy chest comfortingly.

"If only Bootsie hadn't been alone in the house," he said. "Do you know what she told me?"

"What?"

"She said that when he started to choke she ran upstairs to find a first-aid book she knew she had somewhere. She'd saved it from a hygiene course she'd had in college. Then she said when she got up there she remembered that it was in the attic, so she ran up to the attic, and all the time Monroe was downstairs choking to death."

"Poor Monroe."

"If only Bootsie had had the sense to stay *with* him. She could have helped him if she stayed. She could have reached into his mouth and pulled the bloody thing out, for God's sake."

"You mustn't blame her. She thought she was doing the best thing."

"He died all alone. She said when she got back to him, he was dead. His head had fallen forward into his dinner plate and when she pulled it up his forehead was covered with mashed potatoes."

"How ghastly."

"If only she'd stayed with him."

"Did she ever find the book?"

"No. The trunk where she thought it was was locked."

"Oh, Max, I'm so sorry. Your best friend."

"Yeah."

"Well, let's stop talking about it," she said. "It's too depressing. Let's go out. Let's go for a drive."

But he was in no mood for a drive; and it was an hour or more before she could persuade him to get up and dress and go out. As they drove he told her about the funeral, the party, about Freddy, and,

45

ironically, when he pulled into the parking lot at the restaurant where they were to have lunch, the first thing he noticed was Freddy's car.

"Don't expect me to introduce you," he said. "It's bad enough that he snubs *me*."

"What if Bootsie's with him?"

He frowned. "I hadn't thought of that. Of course, she will be. In black, no doubt."

But Bootsie had more sense than either of them gave her credit for. Bootsie was in her own dining room with Marylou Harris, whom she had invited to lunch for the sole purpose of finding out who Freddy was having lunch with, who he had driven to the country to see the night before the funeral. "I'll keep my little antennae out," Marylou promised. "but I swear I don't know a *thing* about it." She was somewhat miffed that Bootsie had summoned her as a source of information rather than of comfort.

The restaurant was not very large and Freddy's massive head was immediately apparent. He was wearing a bright-young-architect costume: a cognac-colored corduroy suit, a muscatel wool shirt, a nubby chartreuse tie bristling with short silvery hairs, and desert boots. The girl opposite him wore a navy-blue suit and a neat white hat. It's Sunday isn't it?, she seemed to say.

Freddy was sitting with his back to the door, and it would have been easy for Max and Louise to follow the waitress past his table without attracting his attention if the girl had not looked up and smiled at Louise. Max, in back of Louise, was thus obliged to nod at Freddy, who had looked up also.

The waitress left them at a table at the end of the room. Max, with his back to Freddy, was not sure whether he hated him more or less for not being with

46

Bootsie. Poor Bootsie, he thought. She is not lucky in love.

"That's Anne Bollinger. Was she at the funeral?"

"At the funeral I don't know. At the shindig afterward I don't know either. I don't know anything anymore."

"She's a cousin of Bootsie's friend, the one who used to be married to George Harris."

"Marylou?"

"Yes."

They ordered their lunch. Max was confused. He ate his breaded veal cutlet slowly, wondering if he had mistaken the car in the driveway that morning. Perhaps it had not been Freddy's after all. But, no. It had been. They were all just too cavalier for a simple old Jew to keep track of.

**4**

The astonishment Bootsie had felt at Monroe's death was wearing off, but an element of regret lingered to forestall the future. She would marry again, and soon, she knew, but she knew it only dimly, as one knows that one will dine this evening. For the time being, the swiftness with which death had come, the absence in it of an aesthetic quality, a poignancy to lend it charm, and most of all her presence in it sobered her and made her think of Roddy before herself. So when Freddy arrived on Thursday morning she was sitting on her cantilevered porch wondering what to do with Roddy. She realized now that she should not have led him to the open coffin for a last look. Monroe had looked so well—not rouged at all, or powdered even—that, ever since, Roddy had been expecting him to come home. Just her luck that Lazarus had lately been the subject of the felt-board lessons in Sunday School. Roddy, it seems, had got it in his head that, like Lazarus, his father would rise again. She sighed and went out to greet Freddy. He was wearing Madras slacks and a white polo shirt with an alligator appliqued on the pocket.

"Yoo-hoo-oo," she called in falsetto through the screen door. It was a little joke they had, born of a mutual passion for Yogi Berra's favorite chocolate drink, but this time he did not respond with his usual spirit.

"Yoo-hoo, Bootsie."

"Do you want one?"

"Not right now."

She examined his face. "Something wrong?" He had never refused a Yoo-Hoo before.

"Oh very wrong, Boots, Freddy's in trouble."

"Come out back and tell me about it." Half-blind from the sun, he followed her little white shorts through the cool dark house, to the cantilevered balcony. She sighed as she settled onto a flowered chaise. She was in no mood to listen to someone else's problems, even Freddy's. She put on her sunglasses, the better to observe him. His hulk as he straddled the steel railing, was familiar and likeable. It occurred to her that he was someone it would be possible to marry. She had not known him for very long, but she had recognized from the start that they were birds of a feather. As Freddy had once said, "People are used to complexity. They've forgotten that the shortest distance between two points is a straight line. But you haven't and I haven't either." It was a point she could easily agree with. Yet it was a characteristic that had maddened Monroe, for he had seen and loved in her a quintessential girlishness, a carefree capacity for fun, an ingenuousness that disallowed knowing the geometry of two points and a straight line. In *his* eyes (not

hers), she had duped him, married him not because
she could not live without him, but because he had
enhanced her image of herself. His earthiness, his
unorthodox education and trade had appealed to her
desire to be unique. Her friends had married lanky
squash players and stockbrokers and regarded her
marriage (as she had subtly taught them to) as having been made in heaven. Theirs, originating under
the auspices of room-mates, mothers, aunts, and
elder brothers, were ordinary, earthbound. Bootsie
had gone out and found Monroe on her own (at a
crossroad, no less, waiting for the light to change),
had raced him down a country highway, paid for the
wagered beer, spun with him to the top of a ferris
wheel, clutched him, screaming, on the roller coaster
at Palisades Park, cheered with him at Aqueduct,
gone honky-tonkying with him—all without suspect-
ing that he also knew his way around a tennis court,
wore hand-made shirts and read Rousseau at night
after he took her home, his mind awash with ideas of
her natural goodness. When he found she was, after
all, a pragmatist, his rage was intensified by the
memory of his idealism.

Now, watching Freddy, she recalled Monroe
again.

"You feel so goddamn repentant, don't you?" he
had shouted at her one morning, beginning to understand her. And she had nodded contritely, fixing her
eyes on her Rice Krispies, thrilled at his anger, hoping to transform it with her charming penitence into
love and forgiveness. But he, with a new, and annoy-
ing, contrariness, resisted her charm.

"You little nitwit, you feel repentant for all the
wrong things. Not because you married me for your
damned dishonorable reasons. Not because you

53

ruined my life; oh no. Because I found you *out!*
Right? Don't start to blubber! Just answer me. Am I
right?"

"Yes," she had sobbed. "Everything would have
been perfect except for that." At that point, he had
walked out. She remembered that he had stayed
away all day. They were trying times, those first few
months of marriage. Things had seldom been that
bad again.

"I'm in trouble, Bootsie," Freddy said, looking not
at her but at the river, two hundred feet below him.

"Money?" He had not yet repaid her the money
she had lent him at the beginning of the summer.

"No. A girl."

She raised her hand to settle her sunglasses higher
on her nose and at the same time to hide a smile.

"It wouldn't be a local number, would it?"

"How did you know?" He was suspicious, yet
awed.

"I have my spies."

"Marylou Harris."

"No. She doesn't know."

"She should. It's her cousin."

"What!"

"I'm serious. I knocked up her cousin."

"Congratulations."

"Thanks."

"When's the big day?"

"What big day?"

"Your wedding."

"Forget it," he laughed. "I'm not getting married." But he had blanched.

"Oh, then you *do* need money?"

"No. Just advice."

"I see. You're not getting married. And you don't

need money, but you do need advice. Well, there are paring knives, and gin, and horses, and . . .

"I know all that. And that's not what I meant."

"What *did* you mean?"

"I mean, what shall I *do?*"

"Abortions are legal. *You* don't have to do anything."

He ran his hands through his bushy hair.

"It's so easy," he murmured, "but I don't think she'd do it."

"There are nice homes for unwed mothers."

Perspiration made his shirt stick to his chest, and sweat drops lay along his hairline, trickling one at a time into his ears. "Don't be funny."

"How far along is she?"

"I don't know. She hasn't been to the doctor yet."

"She hasn't been to a doctor at all?"

"No. But there's no doubt about it."

"I'm surprised at you," she said. "I thought you were smarter than that." He was even surprised at himself, but now that he had said it, any doubts he may have had had vanished. He never questioned his own word.

"I assure you, Bootsie, there's no mistake."

"It sounds like a classic case to me."

"Of what? Getting me to marry her?"

"Yes, or testing you. Can she trust you, is what she means."

"She's not that type."

"She doesn't sound exactly like the heroic type either."

"Heroic. Who's heroic these days? I can see her point." He wadded up an empty cigarette pack and threw it over the porch railing. "But why am I defending her?"

"I might have known no relation of Marylou Harris's could be heroic. But, most men are dumb, like you."

"Ain't so dumb, Boots. Ain't gittin' hitched."

"That's what *you* say." But he would not be goaded, even though he had proposed to marry Anne the night before. He swung his hefty leg over the railing and took a cigarette out of the aluminum box on the coffee table. He never smoked his own, she had noticed, when he could smoke somebody else's. She picked up the box of matches and struck one for him. He settled down again on the foot of her chaise. "You need a shave," he said, running his finger up the inside of her calf. She moved her legs off the chaise, irritated. He took advantage of the extra room to install himself more comfortably against her.

"I'm a rat, but I'm not a murderer. That's my problem."

"It's only an itty-bitty life. Doesn't really count."

"Besides, what if something happened to her?"

"Nothing'll happen. It's safer than having a wart burned off."

"Do you miss Monroe?"

"No. Yes. Let me up. It's too hot." She shoved him away from her and struggled out of the chaise.

He watched her light a cigarillo.

"I miss him," she said. "By the way, speaking of marriage, his friend's getting married. Max Fried. He sounded absolutely ecstatic when he told me."

"I'd probably sound ecstatic too, if I were fifty and somebody still wanted me."

"You don't have to worry. You'll be married in a month and you can be a grandfather by the time you're fifty."

"Thanks."

"Those are the facts of life, Romeo. Girls marry younger every year."

"If only Anne had married young."

"She's not exactly striking you down in your youth. It's time you were settled down."

"Bootsie, lay off. You're making me feel definitely ill. I'm much too young and immature to be a husband."

"And a father."

"And a father. Oooh. I have an awful pain in my gut. Boots, don't let her get me. Take care of me. Don't throw me to the Christians yet. I wanta be a lion for a few more years."

"I take care of you? Do you really want me to take care of you?"

"Yes, please. I'm your little boy. Take care of me."

She observed him for a long moment, as if judging his ability to keep a secret that she knew she shouldn't tell. Her attempt to rein in the reckless impulse was unsuccessful.

"You can get rid of her," she said. "It's what happened to Monroe."

"What's what happened to Monroe?"

"You could borrow my glass froster."

"Your what?"

"My glass froster. It's a new gadget. It hasn't even been marketed yet, but I have a friend who helped design it and he gave me one."

"What does it do?"

"It's a chemical spray that makes cocktail glasses frosty."

"And?"

"And it also gives you a high if you squirt it in

your mouth."

"And?"

"And if you squirt too much of it in your mouth it freezes your lungs."

"So you squirted a big dose at Monroe's lungs?"

"I didn't squirt it, I told *him* to squirt it."

"But how could he be so stupid?"

"He's not stupid. Really, Freddy. You can be too insulting for words. He was just a little drunk, and I told him a squirt of the stuff would give him this really great feeling. Like he was flying. So he squirted it in his mouth and then we started to eat and his lungs froze and he strangled."

"But you didn't mean to kill him?"

"I didn't mean to kill him. And I didn't kill him. He killed himself."

"But you tricked him."

"Our marriage was falling apart at the seams," she said.

"Ever hear of divorce?"

"I don't believe in divorce. It would be bad for Roddy."

"You don't believe in divorce, but you do believe in murder. That's pretty neat."

"It wasn't murder. I didn't know what would happen. I knew what *could* happen. I really only meant for him to get a flying feeling."

"For such a flying feeling they could put you in jail for the rest of your life."

"They won't put me in jail. Besides you're the only one who knows."

"What if I tell?"

"Freddy! Promise you'll never tell a soul."

"I won't."

"Promise."

"I promise I'll never tell a soul that Bootsie Osborne killed her husband."

"Shh! And don't joke about it. It's not a laughing matter. Besides, I most certainly did not kill him. He did it to himself."

"But you're just as guilty of murder as if you told a blind man to take a big step when he's standing at the edge of this cliff."

"I am not. I did not tell Monroe to take a *big* squirt. I just said a squirt. And if he interpreted that to mean a big squirt then that's his own tough luck. My friend who designed the thing said that a squirt would give you a wonderful flying feeling, as if you were on top of the world. He didn't say anything about big squirts or little squirts. He simply said a squirt."

"Well, I guess we know how old Monroe interpreted that simple phrase, but I don't know how the courts would interpret it."

"If you mention courts or jail again, I'll scream. Remember, you promised me you'd never tell."

"I won't tell. Don't worry. But what could have been so bad about your marriage? Other women?"

"Oh, there was that, too." She fell into silence, staring out over the river, hating to talk about it, hating to expose to him the flaw Monroe had uncovered in her, even though it was no flaw in her eyes, hating to confess that she, pretty Bootsie, charmer of men, desired by whole tennis teams, the envy of her Junior League, had been a disappointment to her husband. He had wanted a special woman, an innocent, a ripe womanly woman, a free spirit disencumbered by the world's trappings, a noble savage whom he could build a treehouse for, and he had gotten a wise woman, a pragmatic and cynical woman, a woman who squandered his money and dragged him to parties and wanted only one child and was rude to his aunts. The agony of it all for Bootsie had always been her conviction that she *was* special, and special for him. And yet these special qualities she felt she had he denigrated, could get on without: her position as Captain DeVries's daughter; there were not many of her background who would have given Monroe entry to that society. Her taste, her eye for color, her feeling for line, her knowledge of the region's history, her love for good design. All these she felt she brought to him, a builder, and yet he wanted none of it. The treehouse he had dreamed of became the steel and glass contraption she had egged him on to build for her on the mountain land she had inherited. Oh, yes, he had loved the house when it was finished, acted as if it had all been his own idea, but he had not been able to apply those principles of design and form and space and history she thought she had drummed into his head to his instant neighborhoods on the other side of the mountain, his mean-windowed split levels and anachronistic colonials.

Their marriage had been based on a misunderstanding of her uniqueness. She had married out of the ordinary and had felt extraordinary for doing so. He had deflated her by reminding her that she was not the extraordinary woman he had hoped for, had believed she was. A longer courtship would have shown him this, but Bootsie, sensing he was likely to change his mind, had pulled the whole thing off in two weeks, which really *was* extraordinary.

"It was not a marriage of true minds," she said. "I wasn't what he thought I was."

"Well, you got the last word, didn't you?"

"Let's change the subject."

"It's a nice day, isn't it?"

"It's a very nice day. Please don't ruin it for me by talking about courts."

"I thought you wanted me to change the subject."

"Well, I do. But you've got me all riled up. I have no intention of having this in the courts. I'm going away for a much-needed vacation, and I'm going to find myself a much-needed new husband."

"Gee, if you hadn't told me what you did to your old husband, I'd offer to be your new one."

"You would, Freddy?"

"Sure."

"You're too sweet for words. Give me a little kiss."

"Let's go inside so I can give you a big one."

"Oh, no. It's much too soon, Freddy, love. I think there should be a decent interval, don't you?"

"That's what you said on Saturday night. Hasn't this been a decent interval?"

"Saturday was the funeral. Surely you don't blame me for wanting to honor my husband's memory on the night of his funeral?"

"But this is Friday. It's *been* a decent interval."

An hour later, Freddy called Anne at her office to tell her he had to take a customer out for dinner.

"See," Bootsie said when he hung up and returned to bed. "You're acting like an old married man already. Telling lies."

"I'll never lie to you, Bootsie, if you marry me."

"You'll never lie to me because I'll always know when you're lying, you nasty thing, you."

61

**5**

Anne knew he had lied. She left her office at five o'clock and took the Third Avenue bus uptown, finding the proximity of the other passengers strangely comforting, because she knew that when she left them she would be alone for the evening, perhaps for the whole weekend. It was not a prospect she looked forward to. She controlled an impulse to weep on the shoulder of the kindly woman seated next to her by multiplying twenty-eight and thirty-one, and then realizing it was not a random pair of numbers but their ages, Freddy's and hers, that had leaped into her mind. Panicky, she wondered if the nice-looking man in the aisle would mind if she followed him home. He had a kind face, a normal husbandly face. Would he be shocked if she asked him to take her in for the weekend, see her through the bad time? She decided he would. He was wearing a wedding ring. The other men on the bus, were they all married too? Or were some of them unwilling casualties, like herself, of the New York rat race called finding someone? She got off the bus. Maybe someone would follow *her* home. Hope springs eternal. Man never is but always to be. In real life it happened. A collision of supermarket carts sponsored romance, from missed planes flowered marriage. But her life, she had come to believe, was *un*real in its lack of such happy simultaneities. A pattern fixed in childhood gainsaid good luck with good men.

The day spelled autumn. The last of the sun was warm on her back as she walked down her block. But he had lied. The air was clear and cool, but she had scared him off. She waited dully at the corner for the light to change and when it changed realized it had been in her favor to begin with. She assumed he was with Bootsie.

New York had shed the summer overnight. It was humming this early evening with the energy of autumn—of the first weekend after Labor Day. Summer had drooped and gone. Thousands were hurrying home to bathe and dress and hurry out again to meet a friend or lover for dinner. No one would order a gin and tonic tonight; they would toast the autumn with very dry martinis and finger the hem of the starched white tablecloth while they waited for their oysters to arrive. They would tear a piece of crusty bread in two and dip it into the last of the seafood sauce while they waited for their steaks, and they would talk later over coffee of the concert series they had subscribed to and of renting a ski house in Stowe with the people from the beach house in Easthampton. She bought a can of Beefaroni and waited again for the light to change.

She turned the key in her door and set the paper bag of Beefaroni in the kitchen. It had happened again, but this time she knew she would not let it throw her. She felt calm, only tired, and lay for an hour on the couch until the room had filled with dusk and she had gathered the shreds of the summer's love and decided what to do with them. At eight o'clock, she picked up the phone and dialed.

"Hi."

"Is it really you?"

"Yes."

"How *are* you?" It was not a rhetorical question. He wanted to know.

"Hungry."

"May I feed you?"

"Yes."

"Shall I pick you up?"

"No. I'll come over. In half an hour." She too would unfold a thick white napkin in her lap and order oysters.

A shower and fresh make-up produced in her a feeling of well-being, as did the curious pleasure of hailing a cab out of nowhere, settling into a corner of the back seat, and uttering the familiar address. And, of course, at the bottom of it all was the knowledge that she was not pregnant. Freddy had asked her to marry him, but he had hated to ask. Now, at least, she could act out of strength.

She slipped out of her coat and handed it to him.

"You look great," he said. She smiled. She could always count on him to see the best in her. "You, too." He led her into the living room.

"What happened to Freddy?" He had never met Freddy, only heard her speak of him, and his name dropping into the evening like a bromide wafer into a glass of water startled her.

"He's out of town."

"So Walter gets a chance at bat."

"I didn't think of it that way."

"Which way did you think of it?"

"I just felt like seeing you. You're good for my ego."

"I'm good for everything about you."

She touched his hand. The funny thing was she knew it.

"Are you still getting your head examined?"

She nodded.

"Good. Stick with it. He'll straighten you out about me."

"I never tell him about you." That wasn't true. She had discussed Walter at great length with Dr. Voccacelli, and together they had tried to discover why he had not been able to catch her imagination long enough for her to fall in love with him. At twenty-five dollars an hour she figured she had spent nearly four hundred dollars talking about Walter.

"You will."

"I've told you, I like the sadistic type. You're too nice." They went to an Italian restaurant in the neighborhood and ordered baked clams and cannelloni. He was too nice, too good. It really *was* what was wrong with him. Twice he had aroused a ferocious passion in her by not being nice, by being unavailable when she had called him. Unavailable for days on end. He had found someone else. Frantic, she wooed him back, only to drop him again when she was sure he was once more hers.

He had come to Columbia from Denver in the days before Denver had a smog problem. He was as straight and honest and uncomplicated as the borders of Colorado itself, except for a rather complicated desire to be President. He was a lawyer now and an administrative assistant to the Mayor, the first step on his way to the White House. He seldom talked about his aspirations, but he *had* told her that it was something he wanted to do for his mother.

"What's the worst thing you ever did?" he asked, when the waiter had taken away their plates and brought the coffee. A chip of lemon peel floated in her cup.

"In my whole life?" She thought for a moment. "I once stole a blue comb from Woolworth's. I was nine, and the comb was beautiful. It had little white flowers painted on the rim."

"I said the *worst* thing."

"Isn't that bad enough?"

"No."

"The very worst thing I ever did?" She sipped her coffee, enjoying the citric and the game. "I think it must have been to give an old lady the wrong directions. It was a terribly hot summer's day, and she was picking her way down our street looking for a certain house. We didn't have house numbers. I told her the people lived six blocks in the opposite direction. They actually lived only a few doors down from us. I felt awful afterward."

"That's hardly the worst thing you ever did."

The candle flames flickered, two points of cozy light, illuminating.

"I turned the same paper in for two courses. A paper on religious symbolism in Nathaniel Hawthorne. I got an A on it from my American religion professor and a B from my American lit professor."

"More."

"I commit white-collar crime."

"More."

"I cheat on my income tax."

"More."

"What are you, some kind of nut?" She filled their cups again, careful not to burn her fingers on the tricky metal lid. "What about yourself?"

"We'll get to me later."

"I can't think of anything else."

He sank back into a corner of the booth. "More," he mouthed.

"I once pretended I was pregnant so someone would marry me." she said.

"He couldn't have fallen for it. You're not married."

"He fell for it."

"Did you change your mind?"

"How do you know I'm not married?"

He blanched. "Are you?"

"Why so pale and wan, fond lover?"

"Are you, Anne?"

"No."

"Well, don't scare me like that."

"It serves you right for being so nosey."

"The worst thing I ever did, I did yesterday."

"What was it?"

He opened his wallet and showed her the money.

"You took a bribe?"

He nodded, looking straight at her.

"Who bribed you?"

He returned the wallet to his breast pocket. "A guy, a sort of nice guy, on behalf of his brother-in-law, who owns a milk company. He wants a contract to supply milk to city hospitals.

"How much did you get?"

"One thou."

"That's not much."

"It is if they find out."

"Can you get him the contract?"

"I can help. I'm in charge of reviewing all the bids and recommending the one I think should get it. I don't have the final say, of course, but they trust me, you know, so they nearly always do what I suggest."

"Why did you do it?"

He looked very tired suddenly. "I don't know," he said. "The guy was sort of nice. Young. Not your typical briber. He came and sat down next to me at a counter where I was having lunch. We walked around afterward, and he gave me the money. Cash, of course. I had already read all the bids, and I was going to recommend his anyway, but I didn't tell him that."

"I always thought you were perfect," she said. His crime made him more attractive.

"I always thought I was, too. I always had this great impression of myself."

"I like you better now that I know you're not," she said.

"I'm going to give it back."

"Why?"

"If anyone found out, I'd be finished. Politically and every other way. I'd go to jail."

"Did you sign anything?"

"No."

"Then how would anyone know?"

"They have ways. Marked bills. Bugs. Even the guy's testimony."

"But you said you were going to recommend him before you took the money."

"That's beside the point."

"You're the limit," she said. "Where did you ever get that conscience? Think of it as part of your pay. You don't get that much from the city. This is like a little bonus. You'd make a lot more if you were with a law firm or in private practice. It's not wrong. Everybody cheats a little. Ordinary housewives steal a billion dollars worth of goods from stores every year. A thousand dollars is peanuts. You do good work for lousy pay, and this is just a present that some rich milk company is giving you. There's nothing wrong with it."

"But I have ambitions, Anne. Politicians have to keep their noses clean."

"Since when? Can you name six politicians who haven't paid somebody off in some way or another? That's the name of the game."

"I'm going to give it back. The guy didn't tell me his name, but I'll track him down through his brother-in-law."

"I might have fallen in love with you tonight," she said.

He made a movement with his hands, signifying helplessness. "If you weren't in love with Freddy, of course."

"Of course."

"Are you?"

"Yes."

"Does that mean you're going to marry him?"

"Yes." She took his breath away and then hated him for looking sick.

"When?"

"Soon."

"Is time of the essence?"

"What?"

"Are you pregnant?"

"No, I'm not. Can't you imagine that anyone would want me otherwise?"

"I'd want you any way."

"Well, you just blew it. I can't stand moral prigs."

"I was just trying to be honest," he said, but she had already stood. The evening was over.

**6**

Helen Schade, preparing her solitary Saturday breakfast in the kitchen at the back of the house, was startled to hear a man's footstep on the porch, but she recognized his hatless silhouette through the door window at once.

She turned down the flame under the percolator and went, with some trepidation, to greet him. As she approached she could see his profile through the curtained pane and felt within her what, despite herself, almost amounted to a flutter of cordiality, for he was an attractive man with a stalwart frame and a substantial bulk—a veritable rock of Gibraltar. He wore a cheery red and black lumber jacket and twirled his old felt hat in his hands. He was the picture of vigor with his ruddy complexion and his shining bald head and he greeted her vigorously:

"Helen." She had often noticed how frequently he called one by one's name. "Helen. Good morning."

"Good morning, Max." She waited, not asking him in.

He shifted his weight in a peculiar rudimentary shuffle and twirled his hat once all around. "May I come in?"

"Oh, do." She stood aside to let him enter. "You know this is Louise's Saturday to work, don't you?"

"Yes, indeed I do, Helen. It's you in particular I've come to see." He executed the same shuffle-like step again. "Mind if I just put my hat here?" He set it on an unused plant stand without waiting for her to answer. He rubbed his hands vigorously. "There's a nip in the air today, Helen. You'll be turning your thermostat up any day now. But you don't have a thermostat, do you?" he added.

"No. We've never converted," she said.

"Still on coal. Well, coal is a thing of the past. Gas is the modern fuel."

"We've always been satisfied with coal. Would you care for a cup of coffee?"

"Well, now, don't mind if I do. If it's no trouble."

"It's no trouble," she said coolly, meaning to get across to him that if it had been any trouble she would not have offered. "I've just made a pot for myself."

He sat at the kitchen table and took out his pipe. As he lit it he watched her over its bowl. She hopped spryly about the kitchen getting cups out of the cupboard, pouring a little evaporated milk into a pitcher, crushing out the lumps in the sugar bowl—both ladies took their coffee without—plucking two spoons out of the bouquet on the table. She turned sharply as the first whiff of pipe smoke reached her nostrils and coughed pointedly to remind him that the smoke was likely to bring on her asthma. But Louise had never mentioned her sister's asthma to him—indeed, they spoke of Helen altogether much

78

less than Helen supposed they did—and he did not understand the cough's significance, even when she raised the window behind him.

She sat down opposite him and felt, despite his smoking, a second surge of cordiality toward him; there was something about him, his bulk, his big, open face, his easy manner that made her feel young —indeed, almost childlike—and protected. Yet, at the same time, she felt strangely domestic to be sitting at her kitchen table with him over a cup of coffee. It was almost as if *they* were getting married. She smiled at him and went to fetch him an ashtray, a tiny china ashtray, the size of a petri dish. And he smiled back; it was easy to see that there was not a man about the place very often—at least a pipe-smoking man.

Max was not one for small talk, and so, when he said to her, "Helen, this house is going to be too big for you," she knew she had better be on guard.

"It's always been too big," she said crisply. "It was too big when Father and Mother were alive."

He drew on his pipe, not looking at her. "If you don't mind my asking," he said softly, "what are your plans?"

"My plans?" She did mind his asking.

"After Louise . . . for after Louise and I get married."

His inability to say "for when you're going to be left alone here," his impulse to be kind to her, irritated her.

"Well," she said angrily, "it all happened so suddenly that I haven't had a chance to make any plans."

"Yes. I'm sorry about that. It was sudden."

Any friendliness she had felt toward him had vanished with his reminder that she was now alone, or would be in a matter of weeks. She had no one: no relations, no friends, no one. And he knew it. He and Louise felt sorry for her.

"It was rather a thing for you to do anyway," he was saying, "to go on in this big house after your father died."

"We loved the house," she said quickly, forgetting how very often during the past twenty years they had hated it, denying how they had hated it even as children: the big house that had never rung with laughter, the dark house that the sun never warmed, the inhospitable house that other children had never wanted to play in—that, in fact, their mother had not encouraged games and visitors in—the awkward house where their mother had sickened and died. It was not a lovable house.

But Max was kind. If he had an idea of what the house had been to them, of what, in the long run, they had let it do to them, he did not give a hint of it. He played with her. "A house means something," he said. "It means something if you were born in it."

"My father was born in this house," she said.

He was kind, but he was a business man. "You have thirteen rooms here." After he said it it occurred to him that it would have been more diplomatic, considering the turn the conversation had taken, to have avoided that unlucky number.

She thought he had done it on purpose. "I didn't imagine you were superstitious," she said coolly.

He laughed. "I'm not." And then, to turn the attack on himself, he added, "Jews aren't."

"I don't know very much about the Jewish people," she said.

But he was not there to enlighten her. He drew on

his pipe. "Helen," he said, "you've got a problem."

"The house is no more of a problem now than it ever was."

He set his pipe down sharply on the petri dish and then lifted it again to wave it at her.

"Helen," he said, "I don't like beating around the bush. I came here today for a reason. I'd like to buy this house from you."

She stared at him. "Buy this house? Whatever on earth for?" Even in her eyes the house presented very few possibilities.

He stood up and with the air of a prospective tenant began to walk about the kitchen. She watched in amazement as he rocked gently on a loose floor board, ran a buyer's eye over the antiquated piping system, knocked expertly on an inner wall, chided with a forefinger the superannuated sink and cooking range. What had got into the man?

"What could *you* possibly want it for?" She was still not convinced that he was not pulling her leg. The house had been for sale for twenty years; in those twenty years they had not received more than half a dozen serious offers. Of those half a dozen, one had been rejected as too low; two of the prospects had not been able to obtain mortgages; one had heard that the bridge was coming and had changed his mind a day before the closing; another had backed out at the last minute when several cases of hepatitis were reported in the vicinity and attributed by the local paper to polluted drinking water; and the last, just two years before, had had second thoughts when a black family bought a house two streets away.

She sighed. For years the two real-estate agents with whom they had listed the house had kept the listing in their files. They sent around, or brought, if they thought there was the slightest possibility of a sale, three or four prospects a year, and every Sunday buyer in the county had been through the house, some more than once.

Despite the fact that real estate values had risen steadily, the agents had encouraged the sisters not to go along with the trend. The sisters, of course, had not taken this advice, and had, each year or two, increased their asking price until it was all out of proportion to the value of their property.

It had become a standing joke between the agents, and "Find a buyer for the Schade house yet?" never failed to evoke wide smiles.

"I almost sold it to Louise last month but she didn't think the price was high enough," Cowley would say to Decker.

"Nice thinking, old man," Decker would reply. "I'm on to something pretty hot myself along those lines. They're going to sell the house to me and then I'm going to sell it back to them at a profit."

And so it had gone for many years. Meanwhile, the house had fallen into disrepair and the neighborhood—choice a generation before—had gradually deteriorated.

"What do you say, Helen?"

She was startled. She had almost forgotten that he was there. She peered into his face, searching for hidden laughter, a guffaw at her gullibility. "Are you serious?" His big, honest face assured her that he was.

"I'm prepared to make you an offer."

"Do you know what we're asking?"

He nodded, and she had a feeling suddenly that he knew a great deal about the house; he had known about the coal furnace, the number of rooms, now the price. "Did Louise tell you?" she asked suspiciously.

"I've discussed the matter with Louise."

"She didn't mention it to me."

"I asked her not to until I had talked to you myself."

There was something more to it. He was being evasive.

"I'm prepared to make you an offer," he repeated.

She waited.

"I'll offer you eighteen."

"If she batted an eye lash, he did not notice, and he was watching her intently.

She stood, picked up their coffee cups and moved with them to the sink. There she turned and smiled at him. "Did you say eighteen?"

He nodded, his face strained and serious.

"You must have misunderstood our price then," she said sweetly. "We're asking thirty."

He made a flopping motion with his hand on the kitchen table—a motion like that made by a fish dying on a beach. "I know what you're asking, Helen," he said, "but it's too much."

"What do you mean, too much? This is a big house."

"I know it's a big house. That's why nobody wants it. It's a big, old-fashioned house in very bad condition."

"I beg your pardon."

He had made a mistake by saying that nobody wanted her house, but he defended himself. "It needs a new heating system for one thing, new wiring, for another, and a whole new system of pipes.

"Does it, indeed?"

He did not waver. "The kitchen should be remodeled. So should the bathrooms."

"I didn't realize you were familiar with our bathrooms."

He did not take her up on it. He could see that he had already antagonized her enough.

"Listen to me, Max Fried," she said. "I'll never sell the house to you. Not at that figure. Real estate is high in this town."

"So are taxes," he said.

"I suppose you know what our taxes are too."

He did know, but he kept silent.

"No," she repeated. "I'll never sell this house for less than twenty-eight five." He regarded the fact that she had come down fifteen hundred in five minutes as a good sign, and the ghost of a smile flitted across his mouth.

She noticed that faint trace of humor, however, and it raised in her a deep loathing for him and his humiliating offer. But, despite this, she went on to defend the house and the price they had put on it. "We had window fans made to order for two upstairs windows and two down five years ago and new linoleum laid in the kitchen three years ago and that refrigerator was brand new only last year." She pointed victoriously to their pride and joy. "It's frost free."

"Yes, but you need a new roof, a paint job inside and out, new gutters and leaders, and screens and storms. It would cost fifteen thousand at the least to fix this place up." He had not meant to say so much.

"I suppose your buildings in New York City are kept up in the very best condition."

He stood, "Helen, I've made you an offer. Eight-

een thousand. In cash. I'd like you to think it over."
He held out his hand but she ignored it and he withdrew it as unobtrusively as possible.

He turned and walked toward the front door. He picked up his hat from the plant stand and hesitated at the door for a moment to see if she would see him out. He felt sorry for her, suddenly, and grinned.

"Helen," he called out, "I'll make it eighteen five. A thousand per room, and five five for the property." He opened the door and stepped out onto the porch.

A moment later she stood on the top step of the porch and made after him a sign that had never before seemed appropriate to any occasion in her life.

That afternoon she crawled onto the big double bed in her room and drew an afghan over her thin little shanks. She comforted one little breast with one little paw while the other warmed itself between her knees. She was cold, cold all over. Her bony little feet were cold, her sharp nose was cold, even her backside was cold. But coldest of all were her thoughts.

He wanted something. He wanted something of hers. And he was never going to get it. She would make sure of that.

Max Fried. He had everything, including Louise. He had walked right into her life and taken Louise away. And now he wanted to take her house away. Or maybe it was the other way around. Maybe he was marrying Louise just to get his hands on the house. Well, she would warn Louise. And she, Helen, would talk to their lawyer immediately to find out what her rights were as half-owner, and what his would be as the husband of a half-owner. Ah, he knew a bargain when he saw one. He wasn't a Jew for nothing. And of the two, Louise and the house, Louise was certainly not the bargain.

Helen chuckled softly to herself as she thought of her sister. Lazy Louise. What a wife she would make. Oh, it was good to think of how he would marry her and then find out how much she ate, how lazy she was, what a terrible cook, how she loved to lie in bed. This last brought a frown to her face as she thought of Louise lying in bed—with Max lying there next to her. It was indecent, at her age. They probably won't at first, she thought. They'll put it off for a while. Maybe they never would. They were close to fifty. She closed her mind to the offensive subject. It was a problem Louise would have to deal with herself. No doubt it had occurred to her.

Deals. He had tried to make a deal with her, but she had shown him who had the upper hand. When he realized she would never sell to him, then maybe he wouldn't be so quick to marry Louise.

Oh, she had him figured out, all right. He thought he could buy her out for a measly eighteen five and then live in the house with Louise while she moved out to a two-room apartment somewhere. Well, he was not getting rid of her that easily. In fact, he was not getting rid of her at all. She turned over on her back and clenched her little fists at her side. Shyster, she said to the ceiling. You shyster. You are not getting the best of me.

When Max approached their house the second time that day—this time to take Louise out to dinner—Helen was up in her room watching from behind the faded cretonne, whose refuge was not needed, for neither of them looked her way as they left the house and got into his car. "How can she simper and smirk at him like that?" she said aloud. "It's enough to make them turn over in their graves." She was standing in "their" room, her mother and father's.

When Max's car turned the corner and disappeared, she marched into her own room to return a moment later with a long, brown paper bag. In the bag was a drill. At the foot of her parents' double bed, which also happened to be the exact center of the large room, was a small cotton scatter rug. (Helen knew it was the center because she had measured it that very afternoon.) The room was directly over, and the same size as, the dining room, and in the exact center of the dining room was a chandelier, whose bowl held the corpses of a score of summer insects. The dining room was the pleasantest room in the house, because it faced south and east, and was full of plants, and because there was a commodious and comfortable couch in the bay window that Louise had appropriated for her own and where she and Max often sat talking late into the night, their voices too low for Helen upstairs to hear. Louise, not one to think of taking down the bowl of the chandelier at the end of the summer and washing out the bugs, would never in a hundred years know that a hole had been drilled in the ceiling directly above it.

Helen kicked the rug to one side and screwed the bit in the drill. At the hardware they had flustered her for a moment by asking if she wanted a flat drill, a star drill, a single-flute, a single-twist, or a two-groove. "Just a plain drill," she had said, "to drill through a wood floor." She had left the store with a single-twist and an extra three-quarter inch bit in case she broke the first one. She dropped to her knees, steadied the bit at the target, and started her work. It was easy. As she gathered momentum the little shavings grew up neatly around the bit, and before she knew it, thunk!, the bit disappeared into the dark inches between the floor and the ceiling. She withdrew it, blew the shavings off it, and measured her handiwork. Three-quarters of an inch exactly. She reached into the paper bag and removed a three-quarter inch cork. With a thumb tack she attached a piece of string to the cork, plugged up the hole, swept the shavings into the bag, replaced the rug, and went downstairs to tackle the ceiling.

First she pulled down the shades, then she set up the step ladder and took down the bowl of the chandelier. Carefully she measured the six inches that she thought would be enough to miss the box and the wires. It was hard work drilling with her arms raised over her head and the plaster flaking into her eyes, and she had to stop and rest every few minutes. Dust settled on her hair and whitened her eyebrows and lashes. She drilled and drilled and drilled, the plaster snowing steadily around her. The faster she drilled, the harder it snowed. At last the bit plunged through the ceiling. She withdrew it and clambered down off the ladder, washed the flies out of the bowl of the chandelier and screwed it back on. It covered the hole neatly. She then vacuumed up the plaster dust, put away her tools and went to bed.

Max and Louise followed the waiter to a corner table overlooking the river. It was, curiously, one of the few restaurants in the area that gave on to the river, and thus it was a popular one, though modest, with its checkered cloths and uncarpeted floors. It was not yet dusk, but the Hudson here flowed through the shadow of the Palisades and took on night earlier than the towns lying to the west and north of the cliffs. Far out on the water the last of the day's sun lay tumbling, although the lights on the great bridge had already anticipated its setting.

The river, tidal and salty even this far from the sea, stirred restlessly beneath them, casting its wavelets against the piles whose resins always evoked her childhood and the week spent each summer at Atlantic City. A mile to the north, the bridge was creating itself in its nighttime image against the darkening water. Louise wondered if Helen were watching its metamorphosis. Prospect Street was two miles north, on the other side of the bridge.

"Well, what did she say?" She turned from the river to him, knowing his answer already. Helen's hostile silence had spoken for itself.

"What did she say? She said what we thought she'd say. She wants $28,500. . ."

"I told you she would."

"She'll come down. Don't worry."

"Did you hurt her feelings?"

"Of course."

"Did you run down the house?"

"Of course."

"Did you mention that we're getting married?"

"Of course."

"Oh, Max," she sighed. "Maybe you could find another house."

"Another house another shmouse. That's the house I want."

"Did you tell her what you want it for?"

"Of course."

"You didn't!"

"No, I didn't. But I will. So she can't say I pulled

the wool over her eyes."

"I wish it didn't have to be like this. It's so hard on her."

"Oh, come off it," he said. "You two nutty dames have been in each other's hair for years. You should be glad I came along and put you out of your misery."

"I am glad, Max. You're the best thing that's ever happened to me. But I just wish something nice would happen to her."

"Something nice *is* happening. I'm taking that white elephant off her hands."

"But when she finds out why you want it. Oh, Lord, she'll kill me. I tell you, Max. She'll go straight through the roof."

"It won't be hard, going through that roof." She tittered in spite of herself. The waitress came and took their order. Two Jack Daniels with a little water. Two Cherrystones, two chowders, and two striped bass. He opened their pack of cigarettes. (They bought a pack every Saturday night) and lit hers, then his own.

"You're sure she didn't want to know *why* you want it?"

"Nope."

"She will."

"Well, tell her."

"Not me. You tell her."

"Is it so bad? I ask you, Louise. Is it so bad?"

"I don't think so. But she's different. These things mean more to her. The idea of the family estate being turned into a Jewish convalescent home would just kill her."

"Estate? Don't tell me you have delusions of grandeur, too."

"I was using it loosely. But it was a beautiful house at one time, in Grandfather's day. And it had grounds."

"No more than it has today. I've been to the Courthouse to look at the deed."

"I know you have." She didn't like it much either. "It *was* the best neighborhood in town."

"The second best," he said.

"Some people thought it was best."

"The same people who think their houses are worth $28,500 of somebody else's hard-earned cash."

"Yes." There was no fight in Louise. Never had been. She would agree with anything just to keep the peace. Their clams came and took the edge off their enmity.

"Why don't you offer her more, Max?"

"I would, if I had any more to offer. If I hadn't had to pay Schuler $3,000 to get the damned street rezoned, I would have had that money. I'm not trying to gouge Helen. It's just that I don't have it."

"Isn't $3,000 a lot for something like that?"

"You're darned right it is." He stabbed a clam with the little fork.

"I didn't know you had anything to do with the rezoning."

"Well, they didn't just rezone Prospect Street out of the blue."

"I thought it was all part of urban redevelopment."

"River Street was supposed to be the cut-off point. I had to get them to throw in Prospect."

"That wasn't very nice of Ted Schuler."

"He's not a nice guy. And it wasn't the first time he's had his palm greased."

They observed each other over their drinks.

"They say every man has his price."

"That's right," he said. "And it's not very high in most cases."

"Have you ever bribed anybody before?"

"Are you kidding? Every time I go down to the buildings department I cross somebody's palm with silver. You've got to. You'd never get anywhere with violations if you didn't."

"You mean, in New York City."

"New York City, Iowa City, Sioux City. That's the name of the game, baby. And sleepy towns on the banks of the Hudson are no exception."

"My hands are clean," she said. "I can't help what anybody else does."

"Not even your husband?"

"If it doesn't bother you, it doesn't bother me."

"Two minds of one accord. It doesn't bother me." The chowder was fine and so was the bass.

After they left, they drove to Max's place.

"Take a turn along the beach?" She nodded. He drove down to the sea wall and parked the car. They unlocked the wrought-iron gate and walked down the flagstone steps to the beach. The tide, now ebbed, had left the sand too wet for walking, so they sat on a bench, stolen years before from the town park, and had another pair of cigarettes, their third. A harvest moon high above them raced the clouds across the valley and threw a broad road of light on the river. The cliffs of the Palisades looming to the north formed a backdrop to the little cove where they sat, though southward they were exposed to the river and the score or two of bobbling masts that identified the boat club. Waves, larger than usual, sucked and slapped at the beach, and an east breeze reminded them that summer was over. She drew her jacket, a loose-fitting embroidered Mexican one, closer about her, and settled against him for warmth as much as for comfort. She felt uneasy. Helen was still on her mind, though she was not one, ordinarily, to bother about anything for long. There had been something she had wanted to say to him in the restaurant, but it had slipped her mind. What was it? Oh, yes. The zoning.

"Don't mention to Helen ever about the rezoning, will you Max?"

"No." He flicked his cigarette away. The ash brightened for a moment then diminished. She threw hers after it and watched it do the same.

"She'd never understand."

"I know." Louise could just imagine Helen's reaction. First, she would lace into her. "You senseless, blithering, scatterbrained idiot. How could you let this this *Man* do this to us? You fool, don't you know men like him are doing women out of their fortunes every day of the year? How do you know how many other wives he's had? How do you know what he comes from? Carnival people, for all we know. I'd like to smack you, Louise. Smack some sense in that empty head of yours." Exhausted, her anger would subside, only to sizzle up again like a fresh piece of butter dropped into a hot frying pan. "Don't you *see*, Louise. He wants you for your money. It's sure as shooting he's not after you for your looks, or your youth, or your fancy clothes, or your lazy ways. It's your *money*, fool."

"Oh, Helen, I don't have any money."

"What do you call that account you have in the savings bank? I don't call eight thousand dollars chicken feed. And then there's the house. You'll get fifteen thousand from the house when we sell it."

Louise thought guiltily of her bank account. She had withdrawn it all and put it in mutual funds, on Max's advice.

"He's not after my money, Helen. He loves me." But that verb would only outrage her further. And so it would go. And when her anger with Louise was spent, she would go to the minister for advice, and then to their doctor, and then to their lawyer and together they would put an end to Louise's romance, convince her of Max's low-downness, make her see the light, perhaps even have him served with a summons. No, he must never tell her he had had anything to do with the rezoning of Prospect Street.

"We won't tell her a thing, Louise. I shouldn't even have told you."

She kissed his hand. "It doesn't matter to me," she said. "I suppose in business you have to do things like that." A tanker was passing far out in the channel, its bulk low in the water, lights bow and stern delineating. They sat in silence until its wake arrived with a crash, swell upon swell flinging salt spray and sand in their direction. They left and went to his apartment.

"I still think you should offer her more." She was seldom so persistent. Never, in fact.

"I can't, Louise. I have just enough saved for the down payment and the renovation. The renovation will cost ten thousand." He knelt beside her. "I'd do anything for you, Louise. You're life to me. But I can't pay her much more than I offered. I could go to twenty-one, maybe twenty-one five. But that's the limit."

"Borrow."

"Where? I have no one."

"Bootsie."

94

"Bootsie?"

"Borrow from her and I'll pay her back from my share of what we get for it."

He was silent, figuring. "You have eight thousand in the fund, right?"

"Yes."

"And if I offer Helen $21,500, your share will be roughly ten five. That makes, say, eighteen five. Then you have to pay Bootsie, say, two, leaving sixteen five. That's for our old age. I think we should put the house money into the mutual fund with your eight thousand, by the way."

"Oh," she said. "Is it safe to have it all in one place?"

"Safe as can be. I have ten thousand. I'll need six or seven for the down payment and the closing. Then I get an equal amount from urban redevelopment for renovation. So that makes ten again and we're in business. Louise, you are smarter than you look." His gloom had vanished. He was a new man. A man with ideas paces the floor, stop short in his tracks, retraces his steps, and repeats the performance again and again.

"There are six bedrooms upstairs, Louise, right? And they're big rooms. I get some beaver board or what have you, and partition the rooms so we make twelve rooms out of six. Of course, they can't all use the same two bathrooms. I'll have to put in one extra bathroom. Medicare rules are four to one, I think. A cheap one. No need to use ceramic tile. That vinyl stuff's good enough. Then everybody gets a sink in the room. Slap a coat of paint on and, here's my big surprise, Louise, a real drawing card: wall-to-wall carpeting throughout the entire twelve rooms and hall. How's that for luxury? I have a cousin married to a fellow who installs it. He can get it for me at a good price and help me put it down. When they read wall-to-wall in the ads, they'll be flocking to me. Then the beds. The beds have to be good, because they're in them all day. But furniture's no problem. I'm not worrying about the beds. I've already worked out a deal with a guy I know who auctions estates. Everybody gets a good bed, a not-so-good bureau, a chair, a mirror over the bureau, and what else? Oh, yes, a wardrobe for the rooms that won't have closets after the beaver board goes up. You can run up some nice curtains for the windows, Mrs. Fried, and there'll be new shades all around. A few cheap little lamps here and there and we have it. Oh, we'll need some doilies for the bureaus. Old folks go for that sort of thing. And a vase of plastic flowers for every room.

"Then downstairs," he came and sat next to her on the couch, "downstairs, my blushing bride, will be our rooms, a room for the nurse (the cook will have to live out), and a watchamacallit, family room? A lounge, you know, Louise, where they can all gather and talk and watch T.V."

"But, Max, I thought we were going to live *here*."

"No, there's no sense in running two places, Louise. I'll give up this place just as soon as the house is ready for us. We'll have our own living room and bedroom and bath. The cook can use a little powder room I plan to put in. I guess the nurse will have to share our bathroom, but if you really want to, I'll make you a little kitchen all your own at one end of the living room."

"I don't like to cook."

"Then we won't need that. We can eat what they eat, and when we get tired of it we can go out or get the cook to make us something special."

"I've never shared a bathroom in my life with anybody who wasn't related to me," said Louise.

"Well, it's just the nurse. She has to take a bath somewhere. You wouldn't want me to put in a whole bathroom just for her, would you?"

"No," said Louise.

"Can't you just see it all, sweetheart? It'll be grand. A real going operation. And you know what? I just think I might have that wall-to-wall put downstairs too. How about that? A nice dark green nylon twist. I can get it for $5.99 a square yard, and that's the price for you. We'll slap a little paint on and make it look like a million dollars."

"I forgot to tell you before," she said, "about running up those curtains you mentioned. I wouldn't know how to do that, Max. I've never been handy with a needle."

"That's perfectly all right, Louise. I'm not marrying you to put your foot on the treadle. Maybe Helen will get into the spirit of things and lend a hand. I'll bet she can run up some curtains in no time at all."

"Well, I wouldn't bring up that subject right away, Max. She can be a little touchy, you know."

"She'll come around. I'll have her eating out of my hand before the snow flies."

"What was that you said before about advertising?" He had said so many things; she hadn't taken them all in at first, but now they were surfacing in her mind like flotsam after a storm.

"I'll put an ad in the *Jewish Daily Chronicle*, and a few other places. The news will get around by word of mouth mostly. Of course, a couple of rooms are already taken."

"They *are?*"

"Sure. My mother's sisters. They're old. Over the hill. Can't take care of themselves any longer, though they try like hell. I'm just going to put 'em right in that nice southeast room above the dining room, which, by the way, will be our living room and bedroom."

"That southeast bedroom was my mother's and father's."

"Was it? Well, it's a nice big room. Might even be able to get *three* little ones out of it."

"Let's not tell Helen any of this for a while, Max."

"She doesn't have to know all our private plans. She doesn't have to know anything at all." He moved closer to her on the couch and put his arms around her. She kissed him back, but her mind was elsewhere, and a hundred wishes were flying around in it, a hundred wishes for "something nice" to happen to Helen. The awful burden of guilt, the harvest of desertion, was heavier than she could bear. If only Helen would get married too. She dozed off in his arms and dreamed briefly of a double wedding marred by the objections of the minister and a shrill member of the congregation to Helen's bridegroom, who too strongly, it seemed, resembled her father.

7

Max woke the next morning thinking darkly of
Helen. Women had stymied him all his life. His
mother, his sisters, and his mother's sisters had one
after another laid claim to him, sapping him of his
little wealth, throwing an impassable mesh between
him and success. He had never denied them access
to what he had, and they had never denied themselves the privilege of taking from him. And now
Helen, calling herself a Christian, was holding out
for thousands he could ill spare and getting Louise
upset besides.

He knew he would have to do what Louise had
suggested: pay Helen more and borrow what he
needed from Bootsie. It was not the ideal solution.
Louise would have to use part of her money from the
sale to repay Bootsie, and he had had plans for that
money: Still, there would be enough left. It was the
only way. He threw his legs over the side of the
rumpled bed and sat there for a while scratching alternately his head and his chest.

An hour later his 1961 Plymouth crunched into Bootsie's white gravel turnaround. Coral geraniums bobbed in fine bloom, despite September. Roddy opened the door for him. Once inside, he realized that though he had been in the house last only eight days before, at the party after the funeral, it had in that short time taken on a whole new character. The Oriental rugs were down for the winter and the late morning sun slanted through a window wall of white wool draperies, where in summer nothing at all hindered the breeze from the river or cancelled one iota of the view from the balcony that ran the full length of the house on the river side. He opened the sliding glass doors and stepped onto the balcony. Monroe had had the mountain blasted open to receive his house. Anchored by a miracle of steel, it cantilevered out over the cliff, swaying as subtly as a suspension bridge and giving Bootsie what the editors of one architectural magazine had called the best view in town. They were corrected by Monroe who said that though it was pale beside Big Sur, there was nothing that could touch it in the east.

Hundreds of feet below lay the swift-moving river. Three miles across the water the little towns on the opposite shore presented themselves each in its own perfect forest, or so the miles made it seem. If one could forget even those demure signs of life and if one could blot out the bridge and the river traffic and the trains silently glinting along the east shore and the village directly below one, its waterfront humming now with the activities of a score of Sunday sailors and its streets full of church goers and comers, and finally if one could imagine away the very balcony on which one stood, one could almost believe he was the sole witness of some splendid act of God eons and eons old. It was for this reason that Max liked the view. Monroe liked it for other reasons. After all, he had once told Max, only a rich man could afford such a panorama. And Bootsie, well, living so far above everybody else made Bootsie feel like the queen of some quaint little land, which is precisely how she had early on identified herself to Roddy. When he was five and starting school, she realized he still had this notion in his head, and she was hard put to it to disabuse him of it, so well was it learned.

"Come in to my parlor," she said, opening the sliding glass doors behind him and beckoning with her forefinger. "It's too breezy out there for me."

He stepped into the living room, sliding the doors to again. In her presence, her sociable, fluffy, American girl presence, he felt, as always, clumsy, rumpled, foreign, and dressed wrong for the occasion. Surely he need not have put on a suit for *this* occasion. He should have worn that gaudy golf outfit Monroe had persuaded him to buy only a few months ago (red slacks, white knit shirt with alligator applique), and to complete the *sportive* air, to top it off, or rather bottom it out, his huaraches (though their squeak was rather too assertive for his tastes). Here he was instead in a blue suit that was too big in the seat and too short in the arms.

Bootsie, on the other hand, was wearing exactly what he supposed Vogue magazine would approve a young woman of leisure to wear on a cheerful Sunday morning in September, not exactly widow's weeds, but attractive in its way. Well, he had the middle-aged look and that was that. She was twirling around the room plumping pillows, pulling draperies, touching things, probably to give him the full

103

effect of her costume. Bootsie in 3-D. They sat in matching chairs facing each other across an ancient and beautiful Kirman. The chairs were low and squashy—too low for Max and too squashy, though she had a way she knew was terribly graceful of casting her legs under her so her body formed what she probably thought of as an attenuated Z but what was really, if you wanted to be particular, more like a *lamedh,* not that she would know what that was. A goyische lamedh. He snickered.

"What's so funny?"

"You look very pretty today, Bootsie." She did. She looked like a pretty little fairy (and one would hardly think a so recently widowed fairy), with her fluffy blond curls trembling all over her head and her big black eyes searching his for compliments.

"To tell the truth, I'm depressed."

"You don't *look* depressed."

"Appearances are bewitching," she said, "I mean *deceiving*. Is this a condolence call, by the way?" You couldn't call it that, but what did you say to a question like that at a time like this? You went to see your well-loved friend's widow a week after he had buried him, it was a condolence call, ordinarily. But Bootsie was not your ordinary widow. Or was she? She was pouting now. It was possible. How could he have been so heartless as not to comfort her this week?

"Hardly anyone has come to see me," she said. "You'd think nothing had happened. Freddy has been hanging around, but I sent him away last night. He got on my nerves."

"I can see how he can get on somebody's nerves," said Max. "He certainly gets on mine." He was relieved to hear it. For a while he had thought. . .

"He kept calling me assassin."

"Calling you assassin?"

"And other things in that vein."

"Why?"

"Well, I made the mistake of telling him about something I did. The next time I'll know enough to keep things to myself."

"What did you tell him?" A strange constriction in his chest, or was it his throat? He had the feeling that something dreadful was about to be revealed to him.

"Will you promise you won't tell?"

"On my honor." That isn't much.

"Well, it was really nothing, but he made a big deal out of it. When I found out that his real motive for coming here was to borrow a thousand dollars from me, and for a most disgusting purpose, too, I was so mad I threw him out. But he made off with my money anyway. He needed it to bribe some flunkey in the city government who's supposed to award a milk contract to his brother-in-law's milk company. A common briber I've been entertaining so royally."

"That's disgusting."

"I'm glad you agree. You can imagine how perfectly irate I was when he kept at me about my little sins." She punctuated her sentence with the sharp "tsk" of a lacquered fingernail on a glass-topped table.

"But what was it you told him?" He hated to ask again, but he just had to know. His throat ached like hell.

"What I told him was that in some way you could say that I was responsible for what happened to Monroe. In *some* way, you could say that."

"How Bootsie?" A display of guilt is entirely proper when a loved one is taken suddenly. The comfortable words he would speak were already clamoring in his head, so swift was his relief, but he would let her speak first.

"Well, I know an industrial engineer who designed a gadget that frosts cocktail glasses. This gadget works through a chemical that gives you a sensation of being high, like airplane glue, if you squirt it in your mouth. But it also freezes your lungs, if you squirt too much. Well, he gave me one of these things, and I told Monroe to squirt it in his mouth, which he did."

"And that's what made him choke on the meat?"

"I guess so."

It was really pretty clever, but then Bootsie was a clever girl. The only stupid thing was telling everybody about it. That sort of left her open to blackmail or even to an arrest. She had always been a smart girl—always a little bit smarter than Monroe. First, luring him into marriage when he was getting along fine without it and now luring him into death when he was getting along fine without that.

"I'm really sort of stunned to hear it," he said. It wasn't everyday you met a killer, especially such a cool one and your best friend's wife in the bargain (with the best friend dead, come to think of it). Oh, it was the height of something or other.

She was a forceful person, all right. There was no doubt about that. It was by sheer force of personality that she had kept Monroe by her side these ten years. Max rubbed his temples for a long moment. She gave you the business, Monroe. You never knew what hit you.

"Well?"

Ah, yes. He must say something. She was waiting for him.

"It's a shame."

"What is?"

"Monroe dying."

"It is a shame, but it's not my fault," she said crossly. "I know he was your friend and everything but, if you want to know, he was a beast to me. A perfect beast."

"You knew what you were doing, then?"

"What do you mean by that?"

"You *tried* to kill him?"

"No. Don't be ridiculous. It was an accident." An accident. Just a nasty accident. But did Freud say there was no such thing as an accident?

"If I were you," he said, standing to go, and then sitting down again. "If I were you, I wouldn't tell any more people than you've already told."

"You promised not to tell anyone."

He stood again to go. "Bootsie," he said, "the reason I came here today was to ask you to lend me $3,000, but I'll settle for $2,000, if you can consider it a gift."

"A gift? What does everybody think I am? A millionaire? Monroe's estate hasn't even begun to be probated and already I've been touched twice."

"Monroe's estate," Max said softly, almost to himself. "I miss Monroe."

When he left with the check for $2,000, Max was satisfied. She had a good heart, basically. That he had blackmailed her he supposed had never even entered her mind.


After he left, she wandered out to the balcony. In

the hour past, the weather had changed. The sky and the river now shared a cold gray, the river's portion flecked with white caps.

A storm was coming: her first alone in the house. She shivered. She hoped she had not given Max the wrong impression. Murder had not been in her mind that night. Hers had been a sin of omission rather than of commission. She had simply neglected to warn him of the danger in the froster. Besides, if he hadn't had a pint of Scotch beforehand, his lungs' reaction might not have been so swift or so final. She was not sorry now that he was gone. Rather she was glad. He had squelched her enthusiasms, ignored her ego, insulted her friends, mocked her too often for her to wish him back again. True, she had traumatized him with her artless "confession"; true she had come to scorn his inexplicable passion for bad architecture (the only decent building to his credit was the one he had had built for her to live in); true, they had been ill-matched from the start. But that didn't kill a man. What killed a man was whiskey and greed, and he loved his whiskey and he was greedy, gobbling up the county's farms as fast as they were put up for sale or taxes, gobbling her up the minute she presented herself. After all, he should have seen that it would never work, the two of them. He should have put her off, though admittedly she was not so easily put off. Yes, there had been a moment the night he died, a perilous moment freighted with decisions that should have been made, when she could have said, "Monroe, I didn't mind your leaving the Bollingers' party without me last night, I didn't mind your not coming home last night. I didn't mind your forgetting my birthday last night, I didn't mind seeing your distinctive Landrover parked in Deedee Caldwell's driveway last night when I drove the baby sitter home, but goddamn it, I *did* mind Roddy seeing it there this morning on his way to school. Now be careful. Not too big a squirt." But the moment had passed, her voice had not risen to the occasion, and she had sat there, the slender tines of her silver fork already slipping under a lima bean or two, lifting the buttery morsels to her lips, her eyes watching, fascinated, as his ruddy face, strangely suffused and mottled, crashed into his mashed potatoes. "Yes, I'm glad he's dead," she said to herself, "Let's be honest."

She walked along the balcony to her son's room. He was sitting in the middle of his unmade bed, legs crossed, reading. She tapped on the window and beckoned for him to come out, and in a deck chair built for two she asked him to promise to take care of her, now that his Daddy was gone. The weather made her fearful.

"Read to me, please," he said for an answer. "About the river in the old days." She sighed, picked up a book and opened it to a page marked with a wisp of timothy.

"On this river," she read, "there is great traffick in the skins of beavers, otters, foxes, bears, minks, wild cats, and the like. The land is excellent and agreeable, full of noble forest trees and grape vines, and nothing is wanting but the labor and industry of man to render it one of the finest and most fruitful lands in that part of the world."

"There are still some foxes, aren't there, Roddy, but no beavers, otters, bears, minks, or wild cats, and not nearly so many noble forest trees as there once were." Thanks to your father, she added silently.

109

"Read to me about the Indians," he said. "The part Daddy liked."

She had flubbed it, her marriage, and her failure pricked her now as she read the words he had once read aloud to her, as if to reproach her for her own treachery: "Our Master and his Mate determined to trie some of the Chiefe men of the Countrey, whether they had any treacherie in them. So he took them downe into his Cabin, and gave them so much Wine and Aqua vitae, that they were all merrie; and one of them had his wife with him, which sate so modestly, as any of our countrey women would doe in a strange place."

The words shivered her. It would be a strange place, her house tonight without her husband in it, with a storm coming and his reproach ringing in her ears. Monroe, Monroe, she cried, what did we do to each other.

But she would sit with her son tonight, as modestly as any of her countrey women, remembering a man who had once briefly cherished her.

**8**

By driving very fast, they just made the noon ferry to Fire Island. Anne had meant to spend the rest of the weekend in New York, waiting for Freddy to call, but Saturday dawned too splendidly to squander in her dark apartment. She knotted a scarf around her head and turned up the turtle neck of her sweater as the ferry churned away from the slip. There were only a half dozen passengers aboard besides Walter and herself. After Labor Day the crowds as one returned the island to the sandpipers and the skate, the gulls, the bayberry, and the sea.

The heat of the sun, which had dissipated over the sparkling bay, warmed them again in the lee of the dunes where they spread their blanket and dozed together in an intimacy sponsored by the immensity of the sea and sky, the endless, deserted beach, and the complicated beat of the surf. Dune grasses and bees murmured above them, and the occasional drone of a lazy Cessna reminded her of her childhood, when all planes droned and when all days were as uncomplicated as this one seemed to be.

She turned on her side to look at Walter. He opened one eye and squinted at her, smiling a little. What frightful knot in her psyche had kept her from falling in love with him ten years ago? She would have saved herself so much misery. There was nothing wrong with him. In college she had simply found him too young, too principled, too parochial, too American, too known, too much like the aspects of her own self she was trying to shed. They were cognates, having roots in soil composed of similar elements. He had sniffed her out at that first tea and she had recognized him immediately. Shd had eyed his aura, analogized him to her high-school sweetheart, somehow known without his telling her that he was there at Columbia at great cost to his parents, there to make a name for himself, to reflect glory on them and on the old hometown that had given him a big send-off, write-ups in the paper, a Rotary scholarship, the works. Oh, she knew him, all right. But that was the fly in the pie. *She* was not going to marry someone exactly like herself the minute she got her degree. She was going to make something of herself first, have a career, travel, move in the *beau monde,* make money, hire a decorator to do her apartment and then marry, when she had made her mark, an older man, perhaps a doctor, a neurosurgeon even, or a diplomat.

Those had been her dreams. But what was a biology major to do? She got a job teaching general science in a private school for girls on the east side, made very little money, met the wrong kind of man, moved from one dreary walk-up to another, got her master's degree at night at N.Y.U., and had finally reached the point where she was earning enough money to buy some decent clothes and furniture when she slipped for no reason at all into a depression so deep that she had to seek Dr. Voccacelli's help to get out. He was helping her, but it was hard work. She had seen him only this morning—her first appointment since his August off—and she felt exhausted even now by the great leap forward he had so arduously helped her make.

She had had only a moment to wait in his anteroom before his door opened and his head popped around, like a beady bobbing bird—one of those amusing birds with ether in its head that bobs perpetually into a dish of water. There was something in his bobbing this morning that irritated her—a new sprightliness, as if the month off from all his crazies had done him a world of good. He didn't really care about them, of course, or about her. He just listened to her story and took her hard-earned money. And then went lightheartedly off for a month, leaving her to fend for herself. Well, he would be sorry when she told him all that had happened.

She settled into the plaid wing chair opposite him. She thought it was proof of the mildness of her case that she didn't lie on the black leather sofa where the others reposed to tell him their troubles. She wasn't in that sorry category yet. She was perfectly capable of sitting up like a normal human being and *discussing* herself in a rational, dignified way, like the women in the "Tell me, Doctor," column in the *Ladies' Home Journal*. There was something degrading about lying down to tell all your secrets to a stranger who wouldn't even lie down with you. She wondered if you were supposed to take your shoes off first. Well, she would never know, since he was never

115

going to get her to lie there. Not that he had ever tried, of course. He had merely shrugged when she had announced, that first day, that she would be sitting. "Whatever's comfortable," he had said.

"You're smiling."

"Yes. Such a lot has happened since you left. I hardly know where to begin." She hoped "since you left" hadn't an accusing ring to it. She would have to watch, lest he get the wrong impression.

He waited.

"Well, remember that man I told you I met just before you—just before the last time I saw you?"

"Freddy?"

"Yes." He was wonderful on names, and he never wrote anything down either. "Well, Freddy sort of shaped up into something rather big while you were gone. I mean, I've been seeing him a lot and he has real possibilities." He knew what that meant. She didn't have to explain that Freddy was husband material. That had turned out to be the whole point of her therapy: she couldn't seem to find a man she liked well enough to marry and one who, at the same time, would meet her mother's qualifications.

He looked mildly interested. She leaned her head back against the wing of the chair.

"He's good," she said softly. "I mean sex and all. We swing." She hated herself for using slang. It was a defense that he must easily see through, but she did it every time she talked about sex.

"Is the relationship satisfactory in other ways?"

"Aside from the fact that he's involved with another woman, yes."

Did he look pained? Did it upset him that she had got herself involved again with a man who wasn't going to pan out, who would only hurt her? Well, let him look pained. Maybe it wouldn't have happened if he had been around to help her.

"Is he married?"

"No, but the woman is. Or, rather, *was*. Her husband died last week. Just my luck." She glanced over at him to see if he had smiled at her little joke on herself, but his bland face was vacant, as usual. She picked at a thread in the chair arm, slipped her pinky through the loop. It was all very fine for him to sit there and quietly judge her, as she knew he was doing, but she was the victim of his aloofness. If she felt that he *cared*, perhaps she wouldn't get herself in these fixes. But he didn't care. She represented twenty-five dollars an hour to him, nothing more.

"What are you thinking?" he asked softly. He always knew when she was thinking about him. It was uncanny.

"Nothing." Let him wonder. Her eye traveled over the room, skimming the innocuous Mother and child by a great master (bought at Altman's in a plain wood frame for two dollars; she had seen them there); the black and ecru landscape with its wavy, wobbly trees after Van Gogh, potato-eater period; the African statue in the book case; the neat arrangement of degrees and licenses that was just far enough away so that she could not read the lettering without putting on her glasses, which she was too vain to do in front of him. She had once made out Yalensis on one of them. A Yale man. Well, he didn't look like one. He wasn't the right shape. He was too delicate to have made out well at a rugged place like Yale. Too bookish, too serious. And there was something foreign about him anyway. His coloring, the brown eyes (sometimes so eloquent, but not now), the dark wavy hair (did his wife run her fingers through it?), would not have gone over at Yale. He had probably been an outsider there, made to feel inferior. Maybe he had even gone to the university psychiatrist for advice, conceived a fascination for the beautiful method, gone on to study it, and ended up here in this office judging her, shaking his head at her mistakes after she had left.

"What are you thinking?"

"I'm not thinking anything," she said crossly. But she regretted her sharpness immediately. He was so sensitive. The little flicker of hurt would dart up in his eyes. All right, she would talk, if it would make him feel any better, but *not* about him.

"I don't know what to do about Freddy."

"What do you mean?"

"I have this fear that he's going to leave me. I'm terribly, terribly afraid. He broke a date with me last night and I'm afraid." She shivered. "It's all I think about lately. And I grind my teeth all night. I'm miserable."

"When did the symptoms start?"

"About a week ago."

"Before or after her husband died?"

"At about the same time. I don't remember exactly." What on earth was he getting at? But she knew that he could sometimes ask the most irrelevant of questions and come up with a sweet little association.

"Why do you suppose you fear that he will leave you?"

She slipped her pinky into the loop again.

"I know he will," she whispered. "Everybody I ever loved left me." He sat silently for a minute or two, and then he asked, "Is your fear that he will leave you perhaps (unconsciously, of course), a *wish*

118

that he will leave you?"

"Is that what you think? That I want him to leave me?" She was annoyed. She always hated it when he started creeping up on her psyche with those neatly balanced casebook questions in that cautious tone of his.

"It's not important what *I* think."

No, of course not. Never ask him a direct question about himself. "All right then, why should I want him to leave me?"

"Maybe," he said, "because then you won't have to grapple with the question of marriage, should it come up."

"It's already come up," she snapped. "I *want* to get married."

"Do you?"

She was so tired of these rhetorical questions of his. "Yes I do," she said. "I suppose you think I find someone who's just right and fall in love with him and get all involved with him just so I can be rejected."

"Not exactly as you put it," he said firmly. "But you have repeatedly involved yourself with men who were not free to marry you."

"I don't know why you use the past tense when you refer to Freddy," she said.

"I wasn't really thinking of Freddy when I said that. I'm sorry, of course. Excuse me."

"If what you said were true, I wouldn't have to worry anymore, since Freddy can marry *her* now that Monroe's dead. If what you say is true, I should be glad that I don't have to 'grapple' with the question. But I'm not glad. I'm very unhappy because I know he's going to leave me, and I don't want him to."

"You don't 'know' that he is. You only fear that he is, and your fear is part of your general insecurity. You felt secure with Freddy as long as the conditions that make you feel secure existed, in other words as long as the triangle existed. The triangle protected you. Freddy could not be expected to propose to you, because you both understood that he was involved with the other woman. Now, however, the other woman is free, and the triangle is in danger of breaking up. Freddy is free to choose between the two of you. Although on the conscious level you may wish that he would choose you and fear that he may not, on the unconscious level, you fear that he will choose you and probably give him the impression that you wish that he would not."

It annoyed her that he should feel so free to talk like this about her when he hadn't even seen her in over a month. Or was he so sure of himself simply because her case was so common? When the internist had probed his patient's abdomen and examined his X-rays, he knew at once to say, "A large mass is obstructing your intestinal passage. You are suffering either from adhesions from that appendectomy you had five years ago or from something more serious. We will have to operate." He knew it on sight. It was common. He didn't have to repair to his books, call in consultants, retake the X-rays, make a long-distance call to the famous clinic. No, of course not, and Dr. Voccacelli recognized her symptoms on sight. She *must* listen to him and stop getting annoyed. He was costing her twenty-five dollars an hour.

"Why should I be afraid that he'll choose me?"

"Think of the situation in terms of your childhood," he said patiently. "In terms of the triangle formed by your mother, your father and yourself. You've often spoken of your feelings that they played you against each other, that you were their pawn. You felt weighed down by your responsibility toward them, even as a very young child. You imagined that it was up to you to keep them together, but the only way that you could think of to accomplish this was to strive for their approval, first your mother's, then your father's. When this did not work, when you saw that they were still quarreling, you saw that you could not have them both, and so you chose between them." He paused. "And whom did you choose?" he asked softly.

"My father," she barely breathed the words.

He sighed. Did he feel he was getting somewhere?

"Yes. You chose your father, because, you said, he seemed to need your sympathy and your support more than your mother did. However, you felt guilty at deserting your mother and when they eventually did break up you imagined that, because of your choice, it was your fault."

"Here we go again," she said, "Oedipus. So I was in love with my father. Isn't every little girl?"

"Yes. Every little girl is in love with her father and wants to take him away from her mother. But what happened in your case?"

She looked at him blankly.

"What happened?" he repeated, ever so gently.

"I don't know what you mean."

Although he looked at her with eyes that said "You *do* know. You're resisting," he supplied the answer for her. "You sided with your father, chose him over your mother. But your father turned around a year or two later and left you. You interpreted this as meaning that you and your sacrifice were unim-

portant to him. Moreover, you now had to live with
your guilt not only at have broken up their marriage,
but at having deserted your mother."

"And I've been trying to make it up to her ever
since."

He nodded.

Was he finally doing it, finally helping her to see
the ground-work for the pattern? He still had not got
to the bottom of it.

"Wishes sometimes take fearful shapes," he said.
"Just as your dream of your best friend's death, a
dream from which you wake sobbing and sweating,
may actually be a disguised wish for her death, so,
conversely, your fear that Freddy will leave you may
express itself as a wish, a subconscious one, that he
will leave you."

"I don't wish he would leave me. I want him."

"Fear and desire are often sides of the same coin,"
he said patiently. "It is possible that you may wish
for what you fear, just as you may fear what you
wish for. Let me explain: The sudden death of the
woman's husband has put you in a new position, a
position where you are apt to be rejected but where,
in actuality, you are equally apt to be chosen. You
associate this situation, subconsciously, with the
very similar situation in your childhood. When your
father left your mother, you were extremely upset,
first because you felt that you were to blame, and
second because, soon after, your mother had a ner-
vous breakdown and also 'left' you, for a period of
several months. The present situation, the precari-
ousness of the triangle, recalls those old feelings of
guilt and awakens your old anxieties. You fear that
now you are going to be left again. You protect yourself by *wishing,* and let me emphasize that it is a

subconscious wishing, to be left."

She shook her head.

He sighed again. Perhaps he should not have gone so far so quickly. These young girls who came to him for help with their mixed-up sex lives were a burden, a responsibility he wished he didn't have. He preferred the very nutty to the nearly nutty, the hallucinating manic depressive to the uptight puritan, for that was what this girl surely was. If only they could fall in love with somebody who fit *into* their oedipal pattern instead of always, always with the ones that stirred up that nest of snakes. "Putting yourself, again and again in a position where you are apt to be rejected by men that you love is the only way that you feel you can exonerate yourself for your old guilt. It is only by being rejected that you feel you can make up to your mother and to yourself for your childhood defection."

Yes. It was as clear as a bell.

"It explains your anxiety symptoms," he was saying. "You are deeply disturbed now at the possibility of being accepted, a possibility presented by the unexpected death of the husband, whose existence protected you."

She fell into a deep silence, a silence not of resistance, but of recognition. In it she went back into the primeval ooze of childhood, to the time when she was nine and she had gotten her first, and last, two-wheel bicycle. It was a second-hand bike, all her parents could afford, a heavy, unwieldy vehicle a size or two too large in the hope that she would grow into it before it wore out. (That probably explained why she now bought everything a size too small.) To father fell the task of teaching his uncoordinated little daughter to ride the cumbersome machine. Each evening as soon as supper was over, she would run outside and steer the beast out of its stable under the bay window. Together, reluctant father, eager daughter, and unpredictable steed would wend their way out the driveway, down the hill and across Pine Street to the foot of Bank Street, the long, impeccably flat foot of Bank Street, dead end at both ends. And there, eager, oh so eager to do it right, just once, she would climb onto the seat, place her feet on the pedals, her hands on the handlebars and let her father pull her, like some primitive farmer pulling his primitive plow, up and down the street. For the life of her, she could not manage to give the pedals more than one pump at a time. A half a pump, even a whole pump, but two pumps in succession she could not do. Occasionally, another child would swoop gracefully down out of nowhere, glide, sail to the end of the street, U-turn on a dime and then *standing* on the pedals, arms open, hair and shirttail flying in the breeze, race past again and disappear to some more challenging field. When this happened she would steal a look at her father, plodding gloomily along in front of her, one hand leading the bike by the handlebar, the other clenching and twitching at his side, and vow to be able to do the same some day.

After many weeks of being led from one end of Bank Street to the other, she finally mastered the art of successive pumps, but, alas, she found that she could not pump and steer at the same time, and so her father was obliged to jog along beside her to check the frisky bike when it threatened to wobble out of control. At last after a spring of training came the proud day when she was able to climb into the saddle and pedal off on her own. When she got to the end of the street, she would climb off, turn the bike around, get on again and pedal back to her father, waiting, a miracle of patience, at the other end.

And then, one evening, she decided to surprise him by standing up on the pedals. She climbed upon the seat and waited for him to give the back wheel his customary push to get her started. Whether he pushed a little harder than usual, or whether her steed was feeling its oats she never knew. She only knew that as she tried to raise herself off the seat, she lost control and started to wobble unsteadily toward the ditch at the side of the road. She knew full well what lay ahead, but she had forgotten how to pump, she had forgotten how to steer. She just closed her eyes and waited for it to happen and happen it did. In the ditch lay half a foot of raw sewage, green and putrescent, and in the sewage lay she, with the bike on top of her. Like a wounded animal who turns around to see who has shot him, she turned around just in time to see her father turn his back and walk away.

"What are you thinking of?"

His eyes, so gentle and understanding, were primed with anticipation. No doubt he expected her, in her silence, to have made some brilliant association, to have recovered some long-repressed memory. But she would have to disappoint him this time; she had no new data to feed into his pretty processor, nor had she today a story all rehearsed and ready for the silence she did not care to break with some inconvenient little thought.

"Just about the bicycle and my father," she said. She had already told him the story.

"Yes. A classic rejection."

She wept, more in gratitude for his sympathy than in pity for her own trauma. She was conscious of his watching her closely as she pushed the tears off her face.

"We are all at the mercy of our parents," he had said once in an unusual display of personality.

"I thought I was pregnant," she sobbed, "and he didn't want to marry me."

No response. He was as conditioned in his way as any Pavlovian terrier.

"I suppose you want to play games for a while before you ask me."

"Ask you what?"

"Why I thought I was. How I know I'm not. Aren't you interested?"

"Yes," he said quietly, but she knew that that response too was conditioned. Whoever heard of a psychiatrist answering No to that question?

"Don't exert yourself. Besides, it's not important."

"Not important?"

"My A-Z test was negative."

The small room filled with silence again.

He was one of the most exasperating men she had ever encountered. He was so clinical, so everlastingly conscious of the fact that he was a scientist, a seeker of facts, a tryer outer of hypotheses that he forgot to be a human being. And, for all his learning, he wasn't very learned in any "field" but his own. She remembered the time she had inveigled him into a discussion of modern art, at first simply to get him off an uncomfortable tack he was on and then, when she saw his uneasiness at having waded in up to his chin with a strong undertow making retreat difficult, pursued for the satisfaction of seeing him flounder.

He had floundered all right, but he had gamely trotted out what he knew and tried to follow the leader.

That pitiable stab in the dark, would she ever forget it? "You mean, like Paul Klee's work?" Said with a touch of eagerness. Oh, he had tried to please her, but he had given Klee a hard *e*.

"No," she had said scathingly, "I don't mean like 'Klay' at all. I mean like Kandinsky." And although she had been Teutonic about it, indeed, even viciously so in exploiting the power her advantage had given her, she had been mortified at the same time to have uncovered a weakness in him.

And then there was the time when he had misused the word "secretory." "You're being very secretory today," he had said. She had only barely managed to contain her amusement. Afterwards, in thinking it over, she had been sure that he knew perfectly well that the word did not apply to a condition of reticence; it had been, in short, a beautiful *lapsus linguae* (psychiatrists made them too).

("Do you secrete from every pore and every orifice
Or do you keep it to yourself, reserved, meticulous?
Are you the anal type, we learn, has trouble getting rid
Of all those repressed longings of his naughty infant id?
Or do you ooze and slip about in gay lascivity?
Oh, Doctor Voccacelli dear, what can your problem be?")

"I saw Walter last night. To change the subject." Her voice sounded small and far away.

"Is it a change of subject?"

"What do you mean?"

He closed his eyes and spoke softly. "I'm going to

suggest a couple of things to you," he said. "Just now we talked about how fears might be related to desires. Specifically, that your desire to marry might be inhibited by your fear of rejection, and, conversely, that your conscious fear that Freddy would leave you might be activated by your unconscious wish that he would, a wish designed by the subconscious to spare you the pain of another rejection. Do you follow me?"

She nodded.

"Now," he said, stubbing out his cigarette prematurely, getting down to brass tacks, "consider for a moment that your wish for rejection might actually have become a need for rejection—even a love for it. And then," he said, "and then try to fit Walter into the picture."

In silence she considered it and in considering it she made her leap and grasped the branch of her survival—so that now only hours later as she lay next to Walter she saw him in a new way—as if through a glass plainly.

In the old days Walter had let his moral zeal get the upper hand. A letter-writer, he had made no bones about telling the editor of the *Spectator* what he thought of the cheating that went on at Columbia, of the people who defaced and stole library books, of the perverts in the stacks, the high prices at the bookstore, the bad lighting in Morningside Park. They had called him alternately the conscience of Columbia and the little old lady of Hamilton Hall. And he had indeed been both those things, the darling of the Administration and the butt of a lot of jokes.

Now as she lay sunning in the sand next to him she marveled at how he had changed. Taking bribes!

Even if he was going to give back the money, the important thing was that he had taken it in the first place. He had become complex, had ceased his earnest perambulation through life and had started shoving his way through like everybody else. The bribe made a man of him, elevated him in her estimation. He had learned the name of the game.

Yes, Walter had overcome his predilection for sermonizing. Perhaps he had just gotten disgusted with how little good it did. He was a mellow, more tolerant Walter nowadays, one who had finally learned that nice guys finish last. Some people would be a little disappointed in him, no doubt, if they knew. Actually, she was a little cast down about it herself. Oh, it was a good sign in some ways, and it did put him in a more flattering light in her eyes, but if Walter didn't uphold the law, who on earth was going to? It was really sort of depressing when you thought about it. Depressing and shocking too, as disheartening as turning on the seven o'clock news and hearing Harry Reasoner report that Walter Cronkite had been booked on a morals charge.

Maybe he was changing too much. She did not like the way he had squinted at her just now. He was somehow different today. He had not climbed the five flights to her apartment but had merely pressed the buzzer and waited for her out in the car. He had not carried her straw bag on board the ferry either, nor had he even asked her if she had had a nice time with him the night before. She was used to that kind of treatment from Freddy, but from Walter it was very out of character. She was unaccustomed to his not doting on her.

He had closed his eyes again, shutting her out. She stirred uneasily in the sand. Had her announcement last night that she was going to marry Freddy put him off? What if she didn't marry Freddy, decided to marry Walter instead?

She frowned, and sifted sand. For nearly a decade she had enthralled him, but he was not for her. There was a man waiting for her somewhere who would enthrall *her*, and that was the way she wanted it. She would not have Walter. He doted, and she detested a doting man. Yet today, even last evening, it had not been like that. He had changed in some subtle way. Become independent. She had abused him once too often. He was being nice to her this weekend because he sensed she was going through a crisis. He had probably had other plans for last evening. Maybe he had been invited to a party. She had called *him*, she blushed to recall.

But then, hadn't she a right to? He had sworn his fealty a hundred times. Hadn't he installed the traverse rods in her last two apartments, hung the draperies, knocked down and set up the bed, rolled and laid the rugs, borrowed a station wagon to move her things, made dozens of trips down from her old fifth-floor walkup up to the new fifth-floor walkup with boxes and bags full of dishes, pictures, stuffed animals, the contents of her refrigerator? It's true he had left as soon as his jobs were done, and she had jumped into her new shower to freshen up to go out with someone else, but one could not deny that it was Walter and only Walter she had always trusted to move her stereo set and hook up the speakers, that it was Walter she had always depended on to drive her every Friday out to the Hamptons the summer they both had shares in group houses in Wainscott. And if she didn't meet someone over the weekend, some fascinating one with a car, it was

Walter whom she counted on to drive her back to the city on Sunday. She supposed he was getting back at her now. Glumly, she wondered if he had found a new girl.

Was he through with her at last? Had he taken her last no for an answer? Would he invite her to his wedding? Was he asleep? Pretending to sleep so he wouldn't have to talk to her? Awake, thinking about his new girl?

"Walter?" she whispered.

Walter had made up his mind the last time she had turned him down to forget about her. He was twenty-nine, old enough to understand what No meant. She didn't want him, would never want him, had never wanted him, except as a chauffeur, handyman, bellboy, escort, friend. Six months had passed since that decision. And then her phone call last night. And her peculiar reaction to his confession about the bribe. Was it reasonable that she should like him more because of his lapse? Was it reasonable that graft should titillate, moral fervor bore? Of course it was. He wasn't the first to find that out. Oh, Lord, he breathed, here I am with my love, here we lie on this sandbar, this puny shoal in the Atlantic, this silex in the sea, this speck in your eye. Tell me what to do. Show me how to capitalize on my crime while I have the chance. I know I'm a miserable sinner, God, but if she likes a sinner, show me how to act like one for a while longer. I'll return the money on Monday, if I can track him down by then. Help me, God. She says she's going to marry Freddy, God.

"Walter?"

Play it cool, boy. Play it cool. "Hmmm?"

"I like that sweater you're wearing."

131

Oh, man. Ask, and it shall be given unto you. "Thanks." Don't give anything away. That gets her. That gets her. I knew it would.

"Is it hand made?"

"It looks that way, doesn't it?" Let her interpret that one.

"Have you had it long?"

"About six months."

"Oh, I thought I'd never seen it before. Did your mother make it?"

"My mother! Speaking of my mother, did I tell you that she won a shirt-ironing contest the other day? Ironed twenty-one men's shirts in one hour flat and the gal who placed second only ironed nineteen."

"That's really something, I'd love to meet her sometime."

"Well, not much chance of that. You'll be married in a few weeks."

She hugged her knees and studied the horizon. It was seventeen miles away. She never could remember how they knew that. "I wonder."

He held his breath, stared at the horizon, too.

"Wonder what?"

"If I'll marry Freddy."

"I thought it was all settled." Seek and ye shall find. His heart was beating wildly. Seek and ye shall find. Oh, Anne. He licked his dry lips.

"Oh, it's not positively definite. I mean, lots of things can happen between now and then." She traced a circle in the sand, one cheek on her knee. A strand of blond hair escaped from her scarf. Lots of things could happen. She toyed with a tiny glistening sea shell and wondered, balancing it on the pad of her little finger, how Freddy would react if she told him she was calling off the wedding, Freddy, with his big head of woolly hair, his wet red desirous mouth, his fair skin, so fair his cheeks flamed after shaving as red as a baby's diaper rash. His tender skin was one reason he gave for not shaving as often as he should. The flat black whiskers appeared at random on the alternate days. Not stubbly whiskers but soft and flat and wilted whiskers, clinging to the damp skin of his face. The other reason was his fear of nicking the large aristocratic moles he bore so nobly.

She shivered. He was repulsive. But then, so were most of the men she had fallen in love with. Except Walter. Walter looked like somebody's idea of Mr. Normal American. He was right on the curve. A little taller than the norm, perhaps, a little thinner than the norm; slightly farsighted perhaps, slightly ascetic. He had a murmuring heart that kept him out of sports and perhaps would keep him out of the White House, but he was still on the curve, his physical weakness somehow balanced by his moral strength, by his courage to be bribed and his courage to want to be unbribed, washed clean again. She tried to imagine life with Freddy—life being tromped on, abused, unappreciated, her ego dwarfed by his and mutilated, her neuroses ballooning grotesquely with each new rejection. And then, on the other hand, there was life with Walter—the dimensions comfortable, the proportion equitable, the conjunction correct.

Was she so neurotic that she could come to a fork in her life's road, hold the future in her mind's eye and calmly, objectively, reasonably jettison a chance for happiness? No, she was not. She was not that neurotic. She lay back in the sand and pulled him down toward her. They kissed and then lay with their faces touching, breathing gently on each other, tasting the victory.

"Anne," he said after a while, his voice a little hoarse, "I'm going to give back the money."

"I know," she whispered.

"Will you marry me anyway?"

Her answer was low, inaudible, but he knew what it was. He was too shocked to shout hurrah to the sky. Knock and the door shall be opened unto you. It was written.

They lay in the sun till it had dwindled, and then they climbed to the top of the dune and stood for a moment watching the sky. Surely the horizon was closer than seventeen miles. It seemed to fan out across the marshes and lie there just a mile or two away, peachy and red and attainable. "How's this for walking into a rosy sunset?"

She slipped her arm around his waist and hugged him. "You know," she said, "it feels great to be doing something right for a change."

Freddy took a walk on Sunday night. He left his car at Thirty-ninth Street off Third and started uptown on First. It was a clear night and brisk, but a wind fanned over the city from the east and he smelled rain in it. The river's salt lay light on the air. He bought an apple in a delicatessen on Forty-seventh Street and a bag of M & Ms in a candy store on Forty-ninth. At Fifty-third Street he turned west and walked toward Anne's apartment. She lived at the north-east corner of Fifty-third and Second, over a hardware store. The lights were on in the living room, the dark little living room where they were turned on at high noon to disperse the shadows and scare away burglars, but she had not drawn the curtains over the two windows that faced Fifty-third. She had put a pair of geraniums out on the window sill. Her spirits must be up. She was a strong girl. She could take care of herself. He stood under an arbor of multicolored wooden doors put up by the demolition company that was tearing down the building on the south-east corner and watched her windows, on the second story. She would have more light when the building was down, at least until they put up another in its place, but it was the peculiar architecture of her own building, with the third story overhanging the second, more than the presence of the one across the street that frustrated the sun.

He was immensely glad that he was on the outside looking in rather than in there with her, perched on her tiny couch, while she sewed or read or just sat in her Lilliputian rocking chair listening, smiling, drawing him out. Everything in her apartment was scaled down to make the small room seem larger, and standing he dwarfed even the piano, a spinnet. Everything was small but everything was good. She had made the break with the Salvation Army when she had parted company with her last roommate, and now she had things the way she wanted them. She had a thick rug on the floor, a Bigelow, of course, and a well-appointed hearth where a fire might even tonight, he mused, be crackling. She had two complete place settings of silver, and two on the way to completion, and some nice English china. She even wore good underwear, which was more than could be said of most of the girls he knew, who found nothing to blush about in torn pants and girdles that had long since gone in the seat.

Yes, she had pride, although as Bootsie had pointed out, she was no heroine, which brought him back to the point of what he should do, now that he had so rashly asked her to marry him. He bent and picked up a pebble and, without thinking, threw it at her window. It hit the bottom of the over-hung third story and bounced back to the pavement. He smiled. A hostile action? How would her psychiatrist interpret it? He stooped again, stepped out from under his arbor and aimed carefully. Bull's eye. He returned to the shadows. She appeared at the window, pale and wearing a pink robe, pressed her face to the glass, then pulled the curtains to. A light went out. He should not have done it, he knew; she was jumpy enough as it was. He turned up the collar of his raincoat, crossed the street, and continued his walk, up Second Avenue. His step was jaunty and he held his woolly head high.

"I am a lion," he said out loud. "I am a lion, and ain't nobody gonna put me in a cage."

On Sixty-third Street he walked west again and then up Lexington. A cluster of pretty girls, laughing, fresh, arm-in-arm, turned out of a drug-store and nearly knocked him over. Back to the Barbizon where you belong, he muttered under his breath. "Whoopsadaisy," a chorus, and "Sor-ry," sang one. But another, aloof from the rest and grave, looked into his eyes for an instant. I belong to you, they seemed to say, I understand you. Her somber mouth, the vivid blue vein at her temple, her cropped hair were all that he took in in that instant, but he had dreamed of her before and he was to dream of her again, many times. Tonight, he called her Julia, his mother's name, and she walked with him up Third Avenue and he sheltered her from the wind. He placed his raincoat round her shoulders and pressed his lips to her throbbing temple when she seemed to falter and flag. "My lovely Julia," he whispered, "never leave me."

"You're mine, Robert. I shall never leave you."

"Robert is my brother," he said. It made them both sad, her forgetfulness, but he was pleased, nevertheless, that she did not try to make it up to him. "None of us is perfect," she said in her gentle sad way.

"You are," he said.

He found that he could talk to her more freely than to anyone else he had ever known. She nodded, she agreed, she pressed his hand to her waist in encouragement. She walked at his side in perfect accord, perfect assent; she was all muteness and harmony; yet, before long he felt that she had begun to tug against him in some mysterious way. "Julia, my sweet girl," he cried, "do you love me?"

"I shall always love you, David." But David was his father. "It makes no difference," she sighed. "I love your father, and I love Robert."

"And you love me?"

"I love you."

He was content and at 86th Street they turned east. He bought a hot dog and a paper cone of papaya juice at a stand. He liked the honky-tonk atmosphere of Yorkville and stood in the doorway of a dance hall until the bouncer told him to shove off. He wandered eastward out of the bright lights and away from the oomp-pa-pa bands and the sleek-haired Herren in car coats. A black policeman gave a white Mercedes a parking ticket and a girl in a belted raincoat smiled at him from a doorway. At Second Avenue the street became dark. He slipped his arm around Julia again. In Carl Schurz Park she sat beside him on a bench with her head on his shoulder; together they watched the Pearl-Wick Hamper sign across the East River. The wind was high and the air wet. The park was deserted, the es-planade desolate. Her head slipped down on his chest and then down further. He groaned and settled it gently in his lap. "Comfort me, mother," he whispered. She comforted him and the Pearl-Wick sign twinkled and winked, steadily at first, then faster and faster. Just as it burst into a bloom of pink neon, a voice behind him said, "All right, buddy, you're under arrest."

Freddy jumped up from the bench. Two policemen stood there. "What's the meaning of this?" His voice was thick; his head was spinning.

"What you were doin' is against the law. We're takin' you into the station house," said the taller of the two.

"I wasn't doing a thing. I was sitting here minding my own business."

"You were disturbin' the peace."

"I most certainly was not. Please, officer."

"Tell it to the desk sergeant. Come on, buddy."

"Please, officer."

"Come on, Mac," said the other. "It's quicker that way."

It was a quarter to one, he noticed by the big clock over the sergeant's desk.

"Name?"

"Frederick Pierce Turner."

"Address?"

"333 East 30th."

"Occupation?"

"Architect."

"Marital status?"

"Single."

"What are the charges?"

"He was disturbin' the peace, sarge."

"How?"

There was a pause and then the tall one said,
"He was pollutin' himself."

"Is that true?"

"No," said Freddy.

"Who made the complaint?"

"Nobody, sarge. We caught him."

"You're single?"

"Yes, sir."

"Was anybody around when he, uh, when you arrived on the scene?"

"No, sarge, the park was empty."

"Well, then, how could he be disturbing the peace?"

"Beg your pardon, sarge?"

"If nobody was around to be disturbed, Maculhaney, how can you charge him with disturbing the peace?"

"But, sarge, right in public."

"I don't care, Maculhaney. Get outa here, fella, Beat it."

"Thank you, sir. Thank you very much." Once he was out on the street he ran. He ran like the wind down Lexington Avenue. When he could run no longer, he stopped and leaned against a tree and cried. I'm in trouble, he thought. I'm in trouble. I'm in trouble.

The phrase ran through his mind with a life of its own, over and over again, endlessly and mercilessly. He was in trouble, and not just because his name had almost gone down on a police blotter. He began to walk.

"I'm in trouble," he thought. "I'm in trouble. Something's gone wrong with my life." Tears came into his eyes again. He brushed them away with his sleeve. He had always felt there was something virtuous in a man's tears and had never been ashamed of the fact that he could cry. Tears, redeeming tears. His eyes dried, he walked on, full of high purpose and convinced that he was not yet lost. Anne would save him from himself.

9

The lead story on the eleven o'clock news that same Sunday night was of the hurricane in the Caribbean that had inexplicably changed course and headed for the eastern seaboard of the United States. Anne and Walter had the news on, but they missed the part about the hurricane while they were soaping each other in the shower. Freddy had it on too, but he didn't really take it in because he was rehearsing the new and meaningful marriage proposal he was going to make Anne the very next evening when he took her to Caravelle for dinner. Bootsie went to bed early and didn't watch the news at all. Max and Louise, on the couch in the dining room of 21 Prospect Street tuned in to Channel 2 and learned that the warm moist air of the waters west of Cuba had been forced aloft into the cold surrounding air and had formed an eye that was travelling at 130 miles an hour straight toward them. Max was weary. Louise, uncharacteristically garrulous, had chattered on all through the news about Rosh ha-

Shannah, which they were to observe the next day. *Rosh* means head, in Hebrew, she had informed him, and Rosh ha-Shannah is head of the year. "This is our first New Year together, Max, that first day of Tishri in the year 5722. Shall I blow a shofar for you to summon you to your days of penitence?" "What's a shofar?" "A ram's horn. Don't you know anything?" Helen, who had tiptoed into the room directly above them and pulled the cork out of the floor, heard the news though she couldn't see it. She only hoped the roof wouldn't blow off the house as had happened in '38 and '44 to some of the houses a few blocks south of Prospect Street. Max was hoping the same thing, since a house without a roof wouldn't be of much use to his elderly convalescents.

Helen, lying on the cold, bare and rather dusty floor, wished the news would be over so they would turn off the set and resume the fascinating discussion they had been having about how Bootsie DeVries had done her husband in. She remembered that Bootsie all right. She'd never forget the day she had caught her in the librarian's own private lavatory kissing a boy. You couldn't expect much of a girl who could do a thing like that. Poor fool. Giving hush money to Max Fried who an hour later repeated the whole story to Louise with herself listening in. Not that he knew that, of course. She shivered. It was a chilly night. She should remember to bring a quilt in here with her the next time. Finally Max got up and turned off the T.V. Helen perked up her ears and got into her listening position, which was exactly that of a Moslem on his prayer rug. They were lighting up their cigarettes. She had seen them do it. It was just too cute for words the way they smoked

144

in unison. Disgusting! The way she let *him* light hers in his mouth.

Max settled back on the couch in a prone position with his head in Louise's lap. "Just a few more weeks, dearest," she heard him say.

"Yes," her sister murmured. "Four weeks from today." There was some rustling and grunting as they settled themselves. "Oh, Max," she breathed, "we'll be so happy. It was swell of Bootsie to lend you the money, wasn't it? Now you can pay Helen what she wants for the house."

Helen perked up her ears. Pay me what I want, will he? Well, he may find my price is higher tomorrow than it was yesterday. What's that devil up to anyway? She strained with all her faculties to catch what they were saying, but their voices had become inaudible. At first she was frightened, thinking she had been discovered. Never having been in love, it took her a while to recognize the murmuring quality of its language. Their desultory chitchat, the abbreviations of intimacy infuriated her. What was the use of going to all the trouble and expense of drilling this blasted hole if they're going to sit down there and whisper to each other? She was fierce in anger. Always had been. She had to watch herself or she'd explode, she knew. The smackings of a kiss turned her stomach. How *could* Louise let him kiss her. She had about as much sense as a field mouse. She stood up and brushed the dust and wood shavings off her knees, stuck the cork in the hole and went back to her own room. She would sit up until he left, if she had to sit till midnight.

It was after midnight when Louise crept stealthily up the stairs.

"Don't try to sneak past my door. I've been waiting for you." Fully dressed, Helen stood in the doorway of her room, arms folded in front of her.

"What are you doing all dressed, Helen? Sitting in the dark?"

"Never mind about me. I'm going to get to the bottom of this."

"Of what?" Louise tried to sidle away toward her room.

"Oh, no, you don't. Don't try to put me off once more. You're going to stand here and tell me what you're up to."

"Can't we sit down?"

"If you weren't so heavy, Louise, you might be able to bear standing up for five minutes. All you ever do is flop around from chair to couch to bed and back again. Now stand there for one minute and tell me what you are conniving to do with me and with this house."

"Oh, Helen." Louise was truly wounded. "I'm not conniving to do anything to you." She touched the newel post at the top of the stairs for support.

"I *heard* you, Louise. I heard you talking to him about buying this house."

"But you *know* he wants to buy it. That's no secret. He made you an offer just yesterday."

"Louise, you look me in the eye and tell me why he wants this house."

Louise's bowels swelled and diminished and swelled again. Her face was hot with anxiety, her mouth full of saliva, her head prickling. "Tell me, I said." She looked at her sister, seeing her as if from a great distance. How was it this scrawny little thing could tyrannize her? Why didn't she stick up for herself, tell her sister to mind her own beeswax. Why did she quail like this under her intolerant eye?

What starch she had in her disappeared when Helen went on a rampage. She had to give in to her, had to let her have her way. There was no peace until she did. But this time it was different. This time she had Max behind her. This time Helen would have to pack up and move. Unless she wanted to stay on with the convalescents. A silent titter lit up her eyes. Helen saw it.

"What is so *funny*, Louise?"

"Nothing." She tried not to sound truculent. It would not do to get Helen riled up before Max bought the house. Once he had it in his pocket, then she could tell Helen to go soak her head. Oh, she would let her have it, tell her once and for all what she thought of her. The little Napoleon. She started again for her bedroom.

"Oh, no, you don't, sister. I asked you a question and I want an answer if I have to stand here all night for it."

"I forgot the question."

"I *asked* you, in plain and simple English, why your boyfriend wants this ramshackle old house. You are certainly not planning to have a family, I hope. Or does he have a houseful of brats from some *pre*vious marriage he's just informed you of? Is that why he wants this house? Answer me. Is that why?"

"No, that's not why," Louise shouted. "He's never been married before."

"That's what he tells you."

"That's what I know. Hasn't he lived here in this town for twenty years?"

"We don't know anything about him, Louise. Don't you see?" Her voice was gentler now. She had to make Louise change her stubborn mind.

"Look, Helen. I need my sleep. I am getting married four weeks from today. Yesterday now, because it's after midnight. I have a lot to do and I need my sleep."

"What about me? I need my sleep, too. Do you think I can sleep when this house is being sold right from under me."

"Don't be ridiculous. It can't be sold unless you agree to sell it. Now let me go." She shook Helen's detaining hand off her arm and walked rapidly down the hall toward her room.

"I heard you say Bootsie DeVries lent him the money to meet my price." Helen was following her.

"That's right." Louise plumped herself down on the edge of her bed to untie her shoes.

"Well, there are a lot of unanswered questions connected with that one, but I'll get to the bottom of that later. What I want to know right now, this minute, is why he wants this house. Why?"

"He's going into business, that's why." Louise dropped her shoes and stood up to reach under her pleated skirt and unhook her garter belt. She peeled off her stockings, the belt still attached to them, and tossed them into a chair. "Do you mind? I'd like to get undressed."

"What *kind* of business?"

Louise unbuttoned her blouse and threw it in the same chair, then undid her skirt and let it drop to the floor. As she stepped out of it, she lifted it on the toes of her right foot and kicked it into the chair.

"This street isn't zoned for business."

Louise studied herself in the mirror as she let her hair down to brush it. She had considered having it cut for the wedding, but Max liked it long. He played with it sometimes when they were lolling around in bed of a Sunday afternoon, drawing it all

148

to the nape of her neck and braiding it into a single thick rope.

"Louise," Helen screamed. "This street isn't zoned for business."

Louise walked with as much dignity as she could muster in her underwear to the closet and slipped into her bathrobe. "It depends on the business." Helen flew behind her down the hall to the bathroom. "You tell me what he's got in mind, Louise Schade, you big fat pig, or I'll burn this house down tonight with you in it. Now you tell me. You tell me this minute. I'm your sister here. I own half of this ·house, whether you remember that or *Not,* and I want to know what's been going on behind my back."

"How could I forget," Louise slipped nimbly into the bathroom, slamming the door in her sister's face, and latching it with a dexterity she had seldom displayed before in her life. She had forgotten her slippers and the linoleum was cold on her feet so she pulled Helen's bath towel off the rack and stood on it. She took her time washing, going leisurely over her arms and shoulders, letting down the top of her slip and undoing her commodious brassiere to sponge her breasts and stomach. She creamed her face, brushed her teeth, put on her robe again, hung up Helen's towel, and opened the door. Helen was still there, her face dead white, her tension electrifying the hallway. "The business is," said Louise, weaving her fingers through the tassels on the robe sash, "a convalescent home."

"A convalescent home? Here?"

"He's going to fix it up. Oh, Helen. It's going to be nice. There'll be wall-to-wall carpeting, dark green nylon twist, I think he said, and partitions and new bathrooms. And we're going to paint everything and buy some new porch furniture and there's going to be a cook and a nurse and new beds for everybody and bureaus and lamps. If you could only imagine how *nice* it's going to be, Helen, I know you wouldn't mind."

"Partitions?"

"To divide up some of the bigger rooms. You know, so we can have more people."

"Are these 'people' by any chance going to be Jews, Louise?"

Louise's eyes fell. "Some of them, I guess."

"They don't mix." Helen shrieked. "They don't mix. It's got to be one kind or another. They don't mix."

"Hush, Helen. They mix."

"No. Louise. No. You nincompoop. You nitwit. I know more about them than you do. They don't mix, I'm telling you. They have to eat a certain way. They stick together. Don't you see, Louise. This place will be overrun with them. Nobody nice will come here."

"Helen."

"I hate you! I hate you for being so fat and stupid! What would mother and father say? Do you think they want this house chopped up into little cubby holes for a lot of sick Jews? Do you think that's what they want? We were born in this house. Is that what you want? Is it? Is it?" Louise raised her hands to fend her off. She was right up under her nose, her eyes wild, her teeth snapping dangerously, barking questions, not waiting for answers, crowding Louise too close to the top of the stairs for comfort. "Let's talk about it tomorrow." She side-stepped away from the stairwell and made a dash in her lumbering way for her room. Helen beat on her door with both fists for what seemed like five whole minutes. Then all was silence. Louise stayed awake for hours sniffing for signs of smoke. Helen was perfectly capable of setting the house on fire.

Freddy got all dressed up on Monday night to take Anne out for dinner. Unfortunately, Caravelle was closed on Mondays, but there was a place on Fifty-fifthStreet that was cracked up to be almost as good and it wasn't half as expensive. Not that he was planning to spare the horses. Not tonight. Tonight he was going to ask her to marry him and ask her so she'd know he meant it.

As he stood, curried and oiled, impatient bridegroom to be, waiting for her to open the door, he dwelt with satisfaction on the thought that he would soon be relieving her of walk-ups and dark landings and all that went with them.

"Where have *you* been?" She looked different.

"Fire Island." Her voice struck a peculiar pitch.

"I called you all weekend." Freddy was a stretcher of truth.

"I was gone all weekend."

"Without me?"

"Yes. And I'm not going out with you tonight, Freddy." Her voice. Was it really hers? She wished she had rehearsed this speech, but he had not given her time, having called only an hour ago to say he was coming.

"What the hell does that mean?"

"It means we're through." It was a real pleasure to see that beefy face look pained, to see that fat forefinger fly to loosen the collar strangling that fat

151

neck.

"Now listen here, Anne. I know I'm not perfect; I know I let you down last week, but Christ, you really dumped on me with the news that you were preggers."

"Did I indeed? Well, I'm not 'preggers,' and even if I were I wouldn't marry you. I've changed, Freddy. I'm not neurotic anymore. I'm perfectly normal suddenly and I don't want anything to do with anybody who's not normal."

"What do you mean, I'm not normal?" Oh, Christ. There must have been a police reporter in that station house. It must have been in the *Times* today.

"Anybody who doesn't want to get married is not normal. You are not normal, and I don't want any part of you, because I just discovered that I am normal. I'm fine. I'm not a nut. And I'm going to see Dr. Voccacelli tomorrow and tell him so."

He was actually on his knees before her, hugging her legs. "Please marry me. Marry me, Anne. Give me a chance." His voice was muffled by the pleats in her skirt where he buried his head.

"Stop that. Stand up and act like a man." She pushed him away from her.

"You treated me like dirt for months and now you want me to marry you."

"I love you, Anne. I've changed too."

"Sit down," she said. "I have to make a telephone call before 7 o'clock and I want you to hear it." She picked up the receiver and dialed a number.

"Village Print Shop? This is Anne Bollinger. I ordered 200 wedding announcements last Friday. I *know* they won't be ready for a week. I merely want you to read the copy back to me." She didn't look at him while she waited. "That's right. Now I want one line changed. Change line 5, that's the line with the bridegroom's name, to read Mr. Walter Harrow Mathieson." She spelled it all out for him. Freddy waited.

"What's that supposed to mean?" He suspected a trick.

"It means exactly what it sounds like, Frederick. I am marrying Walter Mathieson whom I've known for ten years and have been too stupid or too neurotic to fall in love with until now. I am no longer a masochist. I've seen the light."

"It's not a joke? Not a morality play?"

"What are you talking about? Can't you understand English? You are being shown the door. Refused. Rejected. Spurned. Replaced. Turned down. Forsaken. Jilted."

"But Walter Mathieson's the guy at City Hall."

"What guy?"

"The guy who said he'd throw a milk contract my way."

"Was that you?"

"Sure."

"Get out, Freddy. Get out of here. And never come back." He raised his arms to ward off her blows. "All right already. If that's how you feel. I'm going. I know when I'm not wanted. And quit punching me." She beat on his back with her fists, and as he stepped nimbly over her threshold she gave him a big kick in the pants.

The shock kept Helen in bed all day, or rather in and out of bed, for she could not sit still. She wandered distractedly around the house, upstairs and down, into the attic, into the cellar, out on the front porch to stare at the river and into the backyard, all the while in her night clothes. Mrs. Potter next door spent most of the day peering through her kitchen curtains. She had never seen such a sight in her life, she said to Mrs. Dorfman, who did volunteer work at Helen's library and whom Mrs. Potter called on the phone every time Helen appeared in the back yard. "It's two o'clock and there she is again in her bathrobe and slippers. Now she's *sitting* on a rock in the middle of the backyard staring up at the house. She's gone round the bend, if you ask me. She's got on a pair of blue flannel pajamas and a bath-robe that looks like it must have been her father's. And a pair of felt carpet slippers. I haven't seen any like 'em in twenty years. Oh! There she goes, in again. I wonder if I should call her sister at work."

Helen stood on the back stoop for a while touching the faded blossoms on the clematis that climbed on strings to the roof and caressing with her palm the worn siding on the house. Then she disappeared inside, leaving the door ajar, though she was ordinarily fanatical on the subject of keeping the doors locked when she was inside.

Louise had gone off to work that morning leaving the radio on in the kitchen. It was tuned to a continuous news station, and most of the news was of the massive hurricane that was hurtling toward New York. Already the temperature and barometric pressure had dropped and the gray skies hung so low over the choppy river it seemed you could almost touch the clouds from the high span on the bridge.

Comparisons were inevitable; the phrases rang in her head. 1958. Winds 60 miles per hour. Tides three to five feet above. Flooding of low-lying areas. Wave-swept roads. Marooned residents evacuated. Coast Guard amphibious vehicle overturned. Crew swept away. Precipitation in a one hundred and twenty mile radius. Thirty-seven power lines and three poles. Waves over power transmitter. Atlantic City boardwalk. Racing waters undermined. Barrier beaches battered. 1944. Tidal waters five feet above. Gusts to fifty. One of the worst. House walls cave in. Nine houses floating in Barnegat Bay. Tides six feet above. Waves twenty-five feet high. Winds eighty-four miles. Seventy houses Long Island. 1938. Winds 500 miles in diameter. Fiercest in years. Six hundred and eighty lives. Cape Hatteras to Block Island. Winds one forty miles. Raking winds. Six point thirty-one inches rain. Eighty mile blasts New York City. Trees toppled by the hundreds. Atlantic City three feet under. Leeward Islands common breeding ground. Landslides along the Palisades.

Helen listened to the storm warnings with one ear and to the pulse of the house with the other. The drip of a faucet, the creak of a board under her restless foot, the scramble of a squirrel on the roof outside her parents' room, the click of the hot water heater in the cellar, the wind rustling the cretonne curtains in her own, the bang of the back door, mail dropping through the slot in the front door. She visited each of the bedrooms, trying to imagine how they would look when he partitioned them, and she sat in the dining room staring at the stained glass set high in the bay window. It was the house's one beauty mark, but today with no sun to bring it to life it looked dull and ugly. The gardenia in the hair of a hag.

It was over. Everything was over.

She wandered out onto the front porch. The river

155

was rising. The storm was due in twenty-four hours, and the river was anticipating it. Tide two feet above. She started down the front steps.

"Excuse me. I must look a sight," she said to two little girls who were passing her gate on their way home from school. "I'm just going down to look at the river." They giggled and scampered off, hand in hand.

"It's going to rain tonight," she said to no one in particular. "We're going to have quite a storm they say. I'm just going to take a look at the river and then I'm going straight home and batten everything down." She lifted her pajama legs and stepped daintily off the curb, looked both ways, and scuttled across the street to the park. "They've let this park go," she called to a woman hurrying by with her shopping cart. "It didn't look like this in the old days. It was kept up to *snuff*." The woman shrugged and passed out of earshot. "Nobody cares any more," Helen shouted. "Everything's changing. Everything in the world's going to pot."

She hurried across the deserted green to the beach. The wind was high at the water's edge, and the spray dancing over the stone jetty made her laugh aloud with pleasure. "I haven't seen it like this since I was a little girl," she yelled. "This is *fun!*" When the wind shifted a little so the spray wet her she shrieked with delight and scampered back out of its range. From her perch on the overturned hull of an abandoned dinghy, she scanned the turbulent water for small craft and semaphored excitedly to a police patrol boat plowing the white caps far out in the channel. "Watch out for submerged logs, captain," she shouted. "Watch out for sea monsters." She laughed delightedly as the wind whipped around her frail form, unraveling the very tie on her bathrobe, then jumped down off the hull and crouched in its lee to play in the wet sand. She shaped four perfect cones with her little mitts and named them Father, Mother, Helen, and Louise, and decorated them with chips of pretty glass and broken shells. "A happy family," she crooned, "a happy family. We are a happy family. Mother makes delicious bread pudding and father takes us all for a drive on fine Sundays. We chug up Main Street in our black Plymouth and when we get to the top we can go in three directions, north, south or west. It's easiest to go west because that's the way the car is pointing and Father doesn't like to turn corners unless it's necessary, but Louise and I beg to go south over the mountain and down the other side to the grounds where one September they had a county fair, a splendid gay fair with cattle and poultry and contests and tents and booths and candied apples and salt-water taffee and a pig named Alice. Alice had seven little pigs and they all looked exactly like their mother. And after we've gotten that far, we wheedle and beg to be driven through the grounds of the state asylum, and there we are very quiet, the four of us, touring bedlam; we are very quiet and still as we take in the mad women shuddering the bars of their cages. Garments flutter from those cages and litter the bushes and lawns below, and empty-faced men sit smoking softly on the benches beneath the trees. The safe ones are allowed out. "Just be thankful you're not in there," mother says, as we drive out through the iron gates. And we are thankful and sober and very well-behaved on the way home. That's our favorite drive, but we like to turn north, too, past the hospital and the high school and the cemetery where lie our grandparents, whose graves, as if they hold something we do not like, we never decorate with flowers. Just as we turn west toward the hills where the apple orchards used to be, we catch a sparkling blue glimpse of the river and listen to Father tell us that it is not really blue, but blue only because it reflects the sky, which, this leads us to believe, *is* really blue. He tells us how the river was in his day and in his father's day and we feel sorry for the poor shad and the salmon that are no more. "Hey," she shouted, spying a group of children down the beach. "There are some other kids. Let's go play with them, Louise!" She looked around. Louise was nowhere in sight. She looked down at herself. "Well, look at me," she said. "I better get back to the house before Louise comes home and finds me like this." Chuckling all the way, she hurried back up Prospect Street, getting there in plenty of time.

School was let out at noon the next day so everyone could get home before the hurricane arrived, and most offices and factories in all the little towns along the river and even in New York City closed early too. Freddy had always wanted to see a good storm from Bootsie's balcony, so he called her up and asked her if he could drive up to see her. She sounded glad to hear from him. Not mad any more. She would be pleased when he told her he was not getting married, after all, and doubly pleased when he told her her thousand dollars was intact. He had gotten it back from the lily-livered clerk at City Hall just this morning, and he had already put it in a nifty little electronics stock selling on the American

Exchange. He was going to double it by Christmas and give it back to Bootsie, taking only a wee little commission for himself.

The scene was spectacular from her front balcony and they had it all to themselves, Roddy having been invited to his cousins' house to watch the storm on television. The wind chased the advance rains in billowing sheets up the river valley and the river itself, swollen by the storm, surged in a thousand new directions. Through her binoculars they could see a freighter far out in the channel, its decks cleared, waves dashing over its prow. The mountain to the north, its southern side scarred by the weather of a thousand ages, was visible, but only barely, through the wall of rain that stalked it. Huddled back against the house, safe from the savage gusts that shivered the very girders whose anchoring Monroe had supervised, they watched.

The storm excited them, their proximity to the elements aroused them and before they knew it they were very nearly naked and making love on the little chintz-covered settee. Afterwards, she sank into a tiny, pleasant stupor, soothed and calmed.

"Let's get married," she whispered.

"O.K." he said. "We make a good couple. I love ya, Boots." She smiled and watched the rain whip along the railing of the balcony. They hadn't even gotten wet. She caressed his forehead with her lips and stroked his back. He was still wearing his shirt. Suddenly she heard the crunch of wheels on the graveled driveway in front of the house.

"Scram," she said, jumping to her feet. "Imperative."

He grabbed his pants and vanished into the house by another door off the balcony. Bootsie pulled her shift on over her head. She slipped into a pair of sandals, and ran her hands through her disordered curls. From the hallway she could see a two-tone green Chevrolet, which she recognized immediately as the village taxi. It idled its motor alongside her aster bed. A small figure stepped up to the screen door and knocked. It looked like the librarian, Miss Helen Schade, but it was hard to tell.

Bootsie put on her condolence-call expression and opened the door for her visitor.

"Come in, Miss Schade. It's so kind of you to come all the way up the mountain on such a bad day."

"I came prepared," said Helen. She undid the chin strap on the old rubber bathing cap she was wearing and yanked it off her head, handing it to Bootsie. "I left my umbrella outside," she said. "Nobody will steal it out of that thingamabob you've got out there, will they?"

"No," said Bootsie. "Nobody will steal it."

"Nobody knows I'm up here," Miss Schade said, kicking off her galoshes. "I sneaked out of the house while Louise was taking a nap." It was chilly, the temperature had dropped into the fifties in the last few hours, but it didn't seem to Bootsie cool enough to warrant Miss Schade's wearing a raccoon coat, especially one that was so *big* on her. Well, each to his own. She dropped the bathing cap on the pile of galoshes, which seemed a good place for it. Just as she did this, however, she caught a glimpse of Miss Schade's lowering brow in the hall mirror. She picked up the cap and set it down carefully on a window seat. She could not help recalling the time when she was in high school that Miss Schade had come upon her in the library lavatory kssing Jimmy

Heaton.

"What are you doing in my lavatory?" Miss Schade had hissed. Jimmy had only been able to grin foolishly, but Bootsie's hand had slipped off the tank where she had been bracing herself, right onto the flush handle. The water crashed and swirled in their midst and Miss Schade raised her hand to strike one of them, she didn't care which one, for defiling her sanctuary. But they had fled and Bootsie had not returned to the library for nearly a decade, or until Roddy was old enough to be taken to the children's corner. By then, Miss Schade seemed to have forgotten, or at least forgiven.

Although she had never been in the house before, Miss Schade made no pretense of having a look at it. Surely she must know, thought Bootsie, if she couldn't see, that it was an architectural oddity: the whole town knew that. As far as Bootsie was concerned, it was the only well-designed house in town; as far as Miss Helen Schade was concerned, it could have been any house. She didn't turn a hair at the idea that she was standing in a glass box cantilevered sixteen feet out over a river two hundred feet below.

"Would you care to take a look at the river from the balcony, Miss Schade?"

"Thank you."

"We have a wonderful view from here, you know; we have a one hundred and eighty degree view of the river."

"Do you now?"

"Yes. We can even see the Empire State Building on a clear day."

"There's Prospect Street," shouted Miss Schade. "I can see my house. I can see it." She thrust the

161

glasses at Bootsie. "Train them on Prospect," she ordered. "Follow Prospect down the hill. Do you see that brown house there with the mansard roof and the double porch? That's mine."

"Yes, yes," said Bootsie, eager to sustain her visitor's good mood. "I see it now. Ooh, it's nice."—Is *that* the old dump Max wants to buy? I don't know now if I should have given him the money.—"Ooh, it's nice," she said again. "I like it."

"Let me see." Miss Schade grabbed the glasses away from Bootsie and trained them on 21 Prospect Street. "I love that house," she murmured. "Look, I can read the sign even. It says 'Water Polluted . . . No bathing . . . by Order of . . . the Board . . . of Health.'" She read haltingly, as if the words were not perfectly familiar. "Isn't that something."

After one more quick look at Number 21, she handed the glasses to Bootsie and marched into the house.

"Where are you going?" Bootsie cried, thinking of Freddy.

"I don't like it out there. It shakes." With Bootsie hot on her heels she marched into the living room and sat herself down on the edge of the couch.

"I came here on business, you know," she said fiercely. "Now sit down over there and listen to what I have to say." Bootsie sat down politely. She couldn't help noticing the blue pajamas that peeked out from under Miss Schade's nice clean overalls.

"Is it true you loaned Max Fried $2,000 to buy my house?"

"I didn't *loan* it to him. I *gave* it to him."

"Aha! Half the battle's won already! I've got you to admit that. Now answer me this: Did you kill

162

your husband with some kind of a glass froster?" Miss Schade grasped the handle of the metal lunch box she was holding on her lap and leaned forward to peer into Bootsie's face.

"I most certainly did *not,*" said Bootsie indignantly. "Where did you ever get that idea?"

"I heard Max Fried tell my sister that just two nights ago. Sunday night it was." She leaned back in her chair. "He said you told him you did it."

"Now, listen here, Miss Schade."

"You listen to me, Bootsie DeVries. I am telling you to get that money back from him so he can't buy my house, or I am going to hustle myself right down to Chief of Police Strange and have you booked for murder. Do you hear me? I am going to do that today. Understand?"

"Miss Schade, I think you're distraught and worked up over this house of yours. I truly do think you are, and I think maybe you ought to consider going away for a nice long rest. Doesn't that sound like a good idea?"

"No. It doesn't. I'm not budging from here till you do what I said. And I'm not budging from 21 Prospect Street. Ever." She faltered. "I'm entitled to stay there." Tears began to run down her cheeks. "Aren't I, Bootsie?"

"Well, of course, you are, Miss Schade." Bootsie knelt beside her and wiped away the tears with the trainman's kerchief Miss Schade had knotted around the suspender of her overalls. "If I hadn't seen you myself yesterday running around in the park in your night clothes, Miss Schade, I wouldn't have spoken quite so frankly about your going away for a rest, but I do think things have gotten the best of you. Now, I'm going to take care of you and get you home where you belong."

"That's what I mean," sobbed Helen. "It's where I *belong*. And now they want to put me out."

"I'm sure they don't want to put you out, Miss Schade, dear. I understand Max is going to start a convalescent home in the house. Wouldn't it be nice if you could be one of the convalescents and just stay on there in your very own room?"

"It's going to be Jewish," she sobbed. "All Jewish."

"Well, Max and your sister are going to live there. *She's* not Jewish."

"They *are?*"

"Why, yes, they are. Now wouldn't you like to stay on there with them and have them take care of you?"

"Yes," Helen said, sobbing anew. "I'd like that. As long as I don't get put out."

"They won't put you out, sweetheart," said Freddy, coming up behind her, looking a little sheepish. "I guarantee you." He put his arm around her quivering little shoulders. "I'm Bootsie's fiancé, Freddy Turner, and I've sent the taxi away and now we're going to drive you home. How's that for a good idea?"

She smiled through her tears, and let him help her on with her galoshes and her raccoon coat.

"Nobody ever called me sweetheart before," she said, putting her arms around his neck and giving him a big kiss.

"We're going to name our first little girl after you, precious; you're the greatest. And we're going to take you out for a drive every Sunday. How's that for a big treat?" She laughed and cried and when she discovered he had a convertible she made him put the top down then and there. She had never ridden in a car with the top down before, and she was in heaven. She sat in the back seat and bounced up and down in the rain, catching rain in her bathing cap and pouring it over herself, shrieking and laughing and bouncing and waving and having the time of her life. The raccoon coat was so wet and heavy when they got to 21 Prospect Street that Freddy had to take it off her so she could stand up and walk into the house. She spent the rest of her years in the house, laughing and chortling to herself in her very own room, which Max left exactly as it was, and they were the happiest years of her life. And every once in a while, Freddy and Bootsie and Roddy and Baby Helen did come to take her for a drive, and Freddy always treated everybody to double-decker ice cream cones before they drove her back home again.

The pulse-pounding sequel to ISLAND FLAME!

# SeaFire

## Karen Robards

*United by passion, they were torn from each other's arms by a nobleman's treachery!*

# SEA FIRE

By
Karen
Robards

**PRICE:** $3.75
0-8439-1084-4

**CATEGORY:**
Historical
Romance

## Love and treachery on the high seas rekindle the passions of ISLAND FLAME'S tempestuous lovers, as their lusty, action-filled romance continues!

**L**ady Catherine had a genteel
British upbringing and was living
happily in America with her
handsome husband and new son.
Jon, her husband, had once
been a murdering pirate with a
quick temper and a fast sword.
If anyone knew, he'd be hanging.

INFLATION $1.50 FIGHTER

LEISURE 1983

ROMANCE #2

# GOLDEN RAIN

## IRENE ROBERTS

**UNBEATABLE BOOKS
AT UNBEATABLE PRICES**

**PRICE:** $1.50  0-8439-1083-6
(cc: 100) 144 pp.
**CATEGORY:** Romance

# GOLDEN RAIN
## Irene Roberts

The tragic accident that killed her parents tore apart the fragile, placid life of Carol Keen. All seemed bleak and hopeless until she met playwright Mark Ransome. He turned her around completely, but left her wondering if love would ever come to her.

**PRICE:** $1.50  0·8439·1081·X
(cc: 100) 192 pp.
**CATEGORY:** Mystery

# SHADOWS
# ON THE MOON
## David Houston

Garth Amesbury was dead, wasn't he? Lots
of people had seen him die — and there had
been that funeral. Of course. But now Tracy
Manning was about to begin a new job as
his private secretary. Her job was to set the
old man's archives in order, but she soon
discovered that the archives weren't the only
things in disorder.

# TOWER AT THE EDGE OF TIME

## LIN CARTER

# TOWER AT THE EDGE OF TIME

## By Lin Carter

*PRICE:* $1.50 0-8439-1097-6
*CATEGORY* Inflation Fighter Science Fiction

Thane was a warrior of blood and steel,
a man of strange powers and godlike form.
To find the secret he was looking for, he
had to cross the Abyss of the Ages and go
where no man had ever been before—and
where none should ever go again.

# *GOLEM* By Barbara Anson

PRICE: $1.50 0-8439-1095-x

CATEGORY: Inflation Fighter Novel

Rabbi Demneck's death looked just like
so many others—an accident.
Then David Demneck, the rabbi's son,
discovered one little clue that said
murder. David's little clue had its roots in
an obscure facet of Jewish law, and it
soon sprouted a vengeance so terrifying
that it threatened to destroy the innocent
as well as the guilty.

INFLATION $1.50 FIGHTER

LEISURE
1094

ROMANCE #3

# PENELOPE DEVEREUX

## SHEILA BISHOP

### UNBEATABLE BOOKS
### AT UNBEATABLE PRICES

# PENELOPE DEVEREUX

By Sheila Bishop

PRICE: $1.50 0-8439-1094-1
CATEGORY: Inflation Fighter
Historical Romance

Charles had won her heart, but he might
have to wait a lifetime to claim her as his
own. Lord Rich could command her flesh,
but he'd never possess her soul. Sir Philip
Sidney was inspired by her to write
beautiful poetry, but could she prevent
his date with destiny?

A POWERFUL SAGA OF HARDSHIP
AND FAITH ON THE GREAT TRAIL WEST

# WAGONS TO UTAH

## CLEE WOOD

LEISURE
1091
$2.25

# *WAGONS TO UTAH* Clee Woods

**F**orced to abandon their lifelong homes in Illinois, the Wheelers forged westward across the barren frontier with few supplies, but complete faith in their deliverance. They were led by the courage and conviction of a man called Brigham Young. The Wheelers were a devout Mormon family. They shared a common destiny, but each had their own desires.

**PRICE:** $2.25
0-8439-1091-7

**CATEGORY:**
Western

INFLATION $1.50 FIGHTER

WAR #1

# WINGED VICTORY

## DAN BRENNAN

UNBEATABLE BOOKS
AT UNBEATABLE PRICES

**PRICE:** $1.50  0-8439-1080-1
(cc: 100) 192 pp.
**CATEGORY:** WWII

# WINGED VICTORY

## Dan Brennan

Just outside Paris lay a Nazi-controlled
industrial complex. The Allies wanted it
bombed before the Germans could use it
against them. The men assigned were the
pick of the RAF. Trained to kill without fear
and destroy with precision, they'd blaze
their way through the night to win their . . .
WINGED VICTORY